•

# THE
# MOMENTUM
## OF
# RED

•

A NOVEL

MONICA KIDD

## POLESTAR
An Imprint of Raincoast Books

Raincoast Books acknowledges the ongoing financial support of the Government of Canada through The Canada Council for the Arts and the Book Publishing Industry Development Program (BPIDP); and the Government of British Columbia through the BC Arts Council.

Cover and text design: Val Speidel

NATIONAL LIBRARY OF CANADA CATALOGUING IN PUBLICATION

Kidd, Monica, 1972–
    The momentum of red / Monica Kidd.

    ISBN 1-55192-682-2

    I. Title.

PS8571.I354M64 2003   C813'.6   C2003-906957-5

LIBRARY OF CONGRESS CONTROL NUMBER: 2004091806

Raincoast Books
9050 Shaughnessy Street
Vancouver, British Columbia
Canada, V6P 6E5
www.raincoast.com

At Raincoast Books we are committed to protecting the environment and to the responsible use of natural resources. We are acting on this commitment by working with suppliers and printers to phase out our use of paper produced from ancient forests. This book is one step towards that goal. It is printed on 100% ancient-forest-free paper (100% post-consumer recycled), processed chlorine- and acid-free. It is printed with vegetable-based inks. For further information, visit our website at www.raincoast.com. We are working with Markets Initiative (www.oldgrowthfree.com) on this project.

Printed in Canada by AGMV Marquis
10  9  8  7  6  5  4  3  2  1

*Contradictory voices tell you who you are.*
— Wallace Stegner


*a scarlet red —*
*red so pure it makes your heart swell*
*with the beauty at God's hand*
— Kevin Major

For Jamie

# Contents

# ✣ *Prologue*

LOVE CAN BE SO FIERCE IT WILL RIP FLESH FROM BONE.

My little girl came into this world glowing with the finality of love, pulled hot and slick from a pool of blood. Her mother lying there, the sweat cooling in the heavy curls over her eyes, her ears, the weight of her sinking lifeless into that steel table, gone from this world. All I could think of was that blistered old statue in the church. Heartsick Mary, weeping at the feet of Jesus. So that's what I named her. I kissed her mother goodbye, hushed my little girl and named her Mary, and took her by the hand into the world.

I knew then that nothing would ever come between us.

·

PART I

# RANDY
# & MARY

·

# ❧ One

"YOU HAVE *GOT* TO BE SHITTING ME."

"Nope."

"He actually compared your jacket to a shower curtain."

"Yep."

"What did you do?"

Mary fished a cherry out of her drink and popped it in her mouth, then flipped her hair behind her shoulders. "I blinked, swung my ass in his general direction, and carried on without him. I think he got the picture."

The three young women shared a look of natural superiority and broke into belly laughs.

Mary and Sara had just finished work at the IGA and joined Tina at The Derrick House for a drink. Tina was still working, and leaned against the glass racks of liquor glowing under a scratched red lightbulb. Mary and Sara sat up at the bar, knees apart and wagging on the high stools, Sara with her Big Rock and Mary with her usual: Jack Daniels, soda and the inexplicable maraschino.

Sara fingered her long brown curls and crossed her legs. "They don't think before they speak, is that it?"

"I suppose," Tina smiled, bending toward the bar for a rag. She began to wipe the counter.

Mary grinned at her. "You look very dramatic doing that. All you need is a thin white T-shirt showing off your chiselled triceps as you stroke up and down, up and down." She demonstrated.

"I save that one for Saturday nights. Makes me look imposing to all the rednecks who come in with attitude. And it ups my chances of getting laid significantly."

"And that's a good thing?" Sara spun backwards on her stool, restless. "The ones you're not related to, no one would take anywhere else. And the others are just waiting for the bus."

"Perfect! Have them for a little midnight snack, give them breakfast and send them on their way with time enough to read the paper before work. What could be better?"

"Hard-boiled Tina." Mary smiled her Chiclet smile. "This bar has made you leathery, deary."

"Speaking of leathery, when are you coming back to karaoke night to get up on stage in those pants?" Tina deflected. Sara nodded.

Mary threw her head back. "I'm still recovering from the last time. Remember that asshole in the corner who kept asking for Dylan? I felt like telling him the first record I owned was *Saturday Night Fever*."

"Harsh, Mary. He was a fan," Sara said, taking a dramatic pull on her beer.

"Some fan. Heckles me when I'm talking, then shouts through my songs."

"I didn't say a fan of what," said Sara, flicking Mary's behind with an attentively manicured middle finger.

"See what I have to put up with?" Mary shrugged toward a man in a dusty ball cap at the end of the bar, who bobbed his eyebrows and pulled a drunken grin. He tried to answer, but cringed at the sound of his own voice and surrendered to the slump of his spine.

"You're cut off, pal," Tina said, then turned back to Mary. "Come on, now, you know you love karaoke."

Mary peered up under her short blonde bangs, then slowly smiled. "Okay, I love it. But don't let it get around. It's part of my mystique."

Sara poked a finger in the air. "Wait a minute. Let me

write that down for when *Rolling Stone* comes calling."

"Or at least *The Western Voice*."

"Piss off, bar-keep. Give us another, will ya?" Mary held up her tumbler and nodded toward Sara's beer.

Tina turned to get a new round as Mary grabbed the TV remote control. Baseball game. Hockey game. Golf game. Weeping ex-lovers in family court. Recreated ancient Mexicans digging up a field. Blue-clad figures huddled in a surgical theatre. Billy Graham. Billy Crystal. She lingered awhile at a panning shot of a Diego Rivera mural, then continued. A cattle auction. Satellite bingo. MuchMusic. She stopped and lay down the remote. Bruce Springsteen.

"Would you *look* at that man's jeans?" Mary said, dropping her chin onto one hand and stirring her drink with the other. "He was a folksinger at one point, you know. Did you ever hear his album *Nebraska*?"

*"Me and her went for a ride, sir ..."*

Sara smiled at the sound of pained crooning just inside the door. Mary turned.

Two men — one drunk, one not — slammed against the door jamb. The taller one caught his jacket on the push-bar handle and grabbed at his companion's shoulder for balance, hauling off the shorter man's shoulder bag and spilling it on the floor. Canisters of film scattered like coins and a news-paper skidded across the dusty floor.

*The Western Voice.*

"You should have left that in the car. It's safer there," the taller one laughed, as he bent to his knees.

"Apparently. We're making quite the impression, asshole," said the other man, looking sideways toward the bar. The women waved in unison.

"Oh, come on. They'll talk about this for years," said the tall man in a drunken whisper that registered just below a yell. He grabbed the paper, shoved it into his back pocket and swaggered to the bar. He placed himself between Mary's stool and Sara's.

"Evening, ladies." The man looked at Mary squarely, his brown eyes glassy. Then he glanced toward the TV. "Bruce Springsteen. Poet laureate of the working man."

Mary grinned under raised eyebrows and exchanged looks with Tina and Sara.

"A toast, then, to class struggle and the eternal search for voice!" He gestured toward Tina as though he were expecting applause.

Tina braved the gap in the conversation. "I imagine I'll regret this, but can I get you something to drink?" The disaster at the end of the bar tried to protest and she shushed him.

Drunk Man turned away from Mary long enough to find his wallet, then he locked onto her again. "A round for my new friends. What are we drinking?"

"I'll have a chocolate martini," said Sara, shooting Tina

a look before she could protest. "And Mary is drinking her regular Cherry Snakebite."

"Mary, eh?" the man asked, his eyes still on her. "Mary, Mary, quite contrary ..."

"Stop there before I have to kill you."

He laughed and shook his head. "Right, then. A chocolate martini and a what? A Cherry Snakebite? That's a bit dramatic, isn't it? A scotch and soda for my friend, and a rye and ginger for me, sweetheart." He handed Tina a fifty.

She took it, handed him the change, downed a shot of tequila and began searching the shelves for a dusty bottle of chocolate liqueur.

"Who are you, and why are you looking at my friend that way?" Sara pressed her finger into Drunk Man's upper arm, and finding it pleasantly ropy, left it there a moment longer than necessary.

He turned his back toward the counter and pulled the leg of his jeans up just enough to prop his booted foot against the bar. Snakeskin.

"Bond. James Bond."

No response.

"Okay. Tough room. My name is Darren Boyce." He paused. "This is where you're all supposed to say, 'You're Darren Boyce?'"

Blank stares.

"I write for *The Western Voice*. Arts reporter. Tough gig.

This fine gentleman at the end of the bar is my dialect coach and massage therapist, Chris May."

Chris nodded and pointed to his vest. "I'm the photographer."

"It was either that, or an industrial-strength fly-fisherman," Sara offered. Chris blushed and Tina passed him his scotch.

Mary leaned toward Darren. "What are you doing out here? That paper's out of Lethbridge, isn't it?"

"Full marks for the pretty one! *The New York Times* couldn't make it, so I have the honour of covering the Juniper Butte Cowboy Poetry Festival."

The women looked at each other. Sara buckled. "The what?"

Darren and Chris exchanged a look that said: *Did we take a wrong turn or have these women never picked up a newspaper?*

After a pause, Tina piped up. "Oh, right! Percy Pennock and his hippie friends organized it for this weekend at his grandad's place over on the correction line. Remember? Bob was in getting propane for that quarter-ton grill of his, and Phil was collecting firewood. He almost tore down my old man's shed for it, the moron." She turned to Chris. "You gotta understand this is the first time anyone's done anything like this around here. I think it's a great idea, but until they actually pull it off, I don't know. Mind you, once it happens, you're going to think the Academy Awards were held right here in the legion hall. We're like that around here."

The photographer smiled.

"Right," Darren spat, trying to master his rubbery lips. "We were over checking out the site this evening. The boys certainly like their whiskey. As do we, I suppose. And now that you know my lineage," he said, turning to Mary, "what's your story?"

"What do you mean?"

"What do you do?"

"I work at the IGA."

"Isn't that precious," he said, smirking.

"That's not the whole story, though," Sara offered. Mary shot her a look.

"No? Come on, then. What's your secret?"

"No secret," Mary said, making a mental note to punish Sara. "I'm a painter."

"Do tell," Darren nodded exaggeratedly. "Maybe you'll show me your paintings sometime?"

"Maybe not," she muttered under her breath, swirling her drink.

Darren turned back to Tina. "We're going to need a room for the weekend. We didn't bother calling ahead, though. We thought we could go on to Stettler if need be. But is there space upstairs?"

Tina smirked. "Oh, just might be. Let me check with the concierge."

"Smart-ass," Darren smiled. "We'll have two rooms, then. Smoking for me. Non-smoking for boy-o, there."

Tina dug around under the counter and found two keys, then wrote the men's names in a forgotten ledger.

"Watch our drinks for us, will you girls? You never know who's out there." Darren winked at Mary, and the men went outside for their bags.

# ❧ Two

IT'S HARD TO REMEMBER THE DETAILS OF MY LIFE BEFORE I met Ros. It's as if gravity in my world worked differently, before her. Other people and their lives pulled me less. She stopped my life on a dime the day I met her in the grocery line.

It was a Friday afternoon, September, combines droning through the front door of the store. The sky was brooding and the radio crackled each time lightning licked along the crest of a hill just beyond the divide, a ridge known to cleave weather systems in two. East and west of it, one county would often lie in sun, and the other, hissing rain: two solitudes. Strange. The farmers of Juniper Butte knew they were safe until the weather broke the divide, and while it held, they drove on like an army, afraid of what rain could do at this point in the harvest. The air was thick with it.

Ros was the new teacher in town, here to replace an old slip of a woman on the world's least likely maternity leave. When the baby was born healthy as the day is long, Ros wound up staying on.

The day I met her, I'd just returned from two back-to-back trips to the valley. I stepped up to the register, distracted by the mental reconstruction of my motor I was currently entertaining, trying to plan a line of attack for replacing the fan that would lose me the least skin possible. A small woman in a toque stood unloading things haphazardly on the counter: artichoke hearts, ground beef, wrapped bologna, four pears, a bottle of rubbing alcohol, a drain plug.

"Little early for a toque, isn't it?" I asked, and readjusted the weight of things in my arms.

She saw my bundle and swept her groceries along, dropping the sawed-off hockey-stick divider down behind them. "I suppose. Saves on shampoo, though." She glanced over my order. "I hope you eat out a lot. You'd get scurvy otherwise."

"Single guys have an enzyme that can turn starch into vitamins. We could eat cardboard and still have healthy teeth and gums." I lay down my canned tomato soup, instant rice, soda crackers and shaving cream, then pulled on the rim of my cap — an old nervous twitch.

"You must live here," I said.

"I'm — what?" She herded her things along. A young girl with gel-sculpted hair and a hickey surfacing under melting make-up rang her through.

"Visitors rarely buy drain plugs."

"Wow. I'd begun to think my phones were tapped and my bedroom wired, with all that everyone seems to know about me. But it saves on small talk, I guess."

"I spend a lot of time on the road. I drive trucks. Gone for a week at a time, usually, but this time, two. Freak frost in Chile."

Blank stare.

"Grapes."

No better.

"I drive produce, mostly. The Chilean grape supply was completely wiped out, so there was a big push on for the Okanagan market."

"Right," she said, and reached for her groceries like a person pretending to listen. She turned. "What's your name, anyway?"

"Randy Thompson. Pleased to meet you." I offered my hand, and she juggled the handles of her bags to free a surprisingly solid right hand. She left and the door closed.

*Grapes?* I thought. *I told her about grapes?* I paid for my complex carbohydrates and wandered home in a daze, the plan for my motor completely misplaced.

LATER THAT AFTERNOON THERE WAS A KNOCK ON MY DOOR.

"You didn't ask me my name," she said, hands in her pockets and jacket zipped up to her chin. A small woman, like I said. Standing on the step below the door, she seemed almost a child. I studied the surprising part in her wavy brown hair a moment before catching myself.

"You didn't give me a chance," I said, pulling the door open and standing to the side. She peeked past me but stayed were she was. "How'd you know where to find me?"

She shrugged. "I went back to the store and asked the clerk."

What a woman. I made a mental note to tip Gracie the next time I was in. "You had me babbling on about the glamorous world of produce transport within seconds of meeting me. Are you a narc?" I smiled and spoke again before she could. "Would you like to come in?"

I watched Ros carefully as she sat on the very edge of the couch, ready to leap to her feet, as though she were afraid of being sucked into it. She fingered the beer I'd produced, pulling off the label in limp strips, which she piled methodically on the crate I used as a table. She had pale green eyes that flashed with yellow in the low sun through the window. She had deep laugh lines. A bump on her nose. A pair of thin lips she worried with square, white teeth. The word for Ros was *glossy*. Her hair glowed as though she'd brushed it for days, and her pale skin — slightly pink with nerves and the beer — was that of a person with lucky genes or one who does a great deal of international travelling. I was fiercely aware of my pitted face and impossible hair, and caught myself checking my socks for holes.

*I'm done for*, I thought.

She talked about her new house, her new job, the comedy of errors in moving from Vancouver to a prairie town of three thousand that didn't even have a bookstore — oh, the horror. She tucked her hair behind her ears, she traced her thumb down the seams of her jeans, she set down her beer and laced her fingers on top of her head. She had the beauty of a young horse, but considering her cultural context, I decided not to share this with her.

By the time the sun set, I was ready to propose.

"I don't suppose you've seen much of our enviable night life, have you?"

She laughed.

"Don't answer that," I said.

She zipped up her coat again and we walked out into the smooth September air. The wind was warm from the west, sucked dry over the Rockies and wending its way eastward through the coulees and over the little glacial hills. The sky to the west glowed red with grain dust and brush fires. Kids howled in the distance, piling on their banana-seat bikes to play hide-and-seek in the dark.

*Yip, yip, yooooo.*

"What was that?" Ros looked up and froze. City girl.

"A coyote." I curled my fingers in my pockets and rocked back on my heels. My lungs burned, all the air gone from them and eddying in the space between us. "It's calling someone back to the pack. Probably a mate."

"How can you tell?"

"Their voices tend to be a bit higher when they're calling pups. Baby talk, I suppose. And they don't move in big packs like wolves. That call was pretty deep, so it must be one adult calling another."

Ros resumed walking. "How does a truck driver know so much about coyotes?"

"We used to hunt them when we were kids. Farmers hate them. I know one guy whose entire year's calves were all bob-tails. The little bastards bite them off. They say it happens when the coyotes go for the kill, but the calf gets away. I call it the coyote's twisted sense of humour, myself. Anyway, we used to get a quarter for every tail we brought back. So I guess you hunt something, and you learn a lot about its ways."

She pushed her hands deeper in her coat and kept walking.

"Did I say something wrong? Oh, my God, you're not a vegetarian, are you?"

She snorted and shivered. "No."

We walked for a few moments in silence.

"*Canis latrans*. About the size of a German shepherd, but half the weight. You can tell what he is at a distance because he's usually long, and keeps his tail down while he runs, not like the wolf and the domestic dog. He's considered by some to be the smartest animal on earth. Mates for life. The more coyotes in an area being hunted, the more of their pups survive. Any sign of danger, and the pack'll just up and move under the cover of night."

What was I doing? Two minutes of uncomfortable stillness had turned me into Lorne Greene. We walked up the steps of the Derrick House, through the doors, and sat down at a table away from the door.

I couldn't seem to help myself. "The coyote is uncanny at adapting to any situation. But he's got two weaknesses. He's a sound sleeper, and he looks back while fleeing."

The waitress appeared, took our order, winked at me and snuck away with a grin.

Ros smiled and looked down shyly. "He sounds like a good survivor, our friend the coyote."

"Best there is," I nodded. "Which is why, despite my early attempts at extermination, there are twice as many now as there ever were."

Our drinks arrived, and Ros took a long pull of her beer. She set it down in front of her and played with the label again.

"Am I making you nervous?"

"Why?"

"No reason." *Help me*, I thought.

She held my gaze awhile, then resumed her study of the beer label. A full two minutes passed while I counted squares on the parquet dance floor.

"I haven't told you the whole story about how I found myself here."

I leaned back in my chair. "Oh?" I tried not to sound desperately interested.

"Promise you'll keep this to yourself?" She paused to reconsider, then started again. "I'd just as soon this didn't get around. I'm trying to make a clean start here."

I shrugged and nodded encouragingly. She shook her hair away from her face and leaned up closer to me, the flame from a tea candle lighting the underside of her chin. She turned side-on to me, and pointed to her right eyebrow.

"See this?"

A tiny scar.

"I wasn't allowed to leave the house to get it stitched up." Her eyes found the middle distance and she rocked forward slightly, withdrawing into a too-familiar geography. "See this?" she asked, persisting in middle distance.

The bump on her nose.

"My nose bled for three days. I had to tell people I'd fallen in the bathtub." Another gentle rock backwards and forwards.

She rolled back her sleeve to reveal a deep purple halo, not long healed.

"A cigarette. My going-away present. Something to remember him by."

She buttoned up her sleeve, tucked her hair behind her ear again and settled back into her chair.

"It's okay. I packed up and left under the cover of night. Only I didn't look back while I was fleeing."

Later, as she lay sleeping beside me, I traced the curve of her cheek, the slope of her throat, the dip under her collarbone. I drank her in and committed her to memory.

Coyotes mate for life. They survive. And they defend viciously what is their own.

## ৵ৎ *Three*

SATURDAY MORNING DAWNED SHAMELESSLY, THE SUN roaming the open fields. People stirred in their beds, happy even before they woke; dogs on back steps winked awake. Around town, the sounds of quiet feet on warming floors, the smells of coffee and bacon. Crows cawed to aloof trees. A morning for poetry.

Mary and Sara found their way to the festival grounds around ten. Like circus hands in a sleepy town, the men went about their business silently, importantly. The old corral made a natural stage. Judging by the few chairs ringing the inside, the organizers clearly expected most people to perch on the fence. Over by the barn, where Percy Pennock used to stoke a fire for his branding irons, the guys had set up a tripod of stripped poplar trunks. From the centre hung a heavy chain about waist-high. Two men bent to lift a heavy iron cauldron into place: the chili pot.

"These guys don't mess around do they?" Sara nudged Mary.

"Curling season's over. They need something to do."

There was a crunch of tires on gravel as Bob Baumgaurt backed up toward the barn with his grill. He stopped the truck and jumped out of the cab, clearing the running boards altogether.

"Hello girls, here to work, are ya? There are three sixty-pound propane tanks in the back here that need setting up, and a case of tomatoes that need slicing." He smiled and kicked a boot up on the bumper, raked his fingers through his hair and replaced his cap. He squinted into the sun. "Real blue blazer today. Where's the third musketeer?"

"I believe she'll be serving breakfast right about now." Mary curled her knuckles into the back pockets of her jeans. "Two guys from *The Western Voice* showed up at the bar last night. They're here for this event, as a matter of fact. One of them charmed his way right into Tina's bed."

"Charmed? Like a fly charms a spider, I daresay."

Mary provided the expected indignant look, then snorted.

"And what about the other one?"

"The other one," Sara offered, "was in rut for our dear Mary here, but the poor thing stalled out after a few whiskeys. I think Percy and them had him sauced before he showed up in town. Poor bastard's gotta work today. He's a reporter. The other guy's a photographer."

"That's enough about my mother." Darren ambled up to the group, his hand shielding his eyes from the sun despite the dark sunglasses he wore. "And don't worry, my liver is the best part of me. I was up with the squirrels this morning."

Sara blushed.

"No squirrels around here," Mary offered.

"Well, I must have them confused with the mice in the walls of your fine hotel."

"Not my hotel. Anyone within fifty miles of this place knows it's better to sleep in the ditch than in that pit."

"Thanks for warning me."

"I figured with the state you were in, the ditch would be too good for you."

"Well, maybe if I'm better behaved tonight I can find more welcoming accommodation."

"Plenty of ditches, I suppose."

Sara backhanded Bob across the shoulder. "See what I mean? Rut. Snorting, shameless rut."

"My dear, don't you worry," Darren said, and sidled up close to Sara. "There's plenty to go around." He turned on the heels of his snakeskin boots and left with a greasy grin.

"Charming fella," Bob snickered, pulling himself up into the back of his truck. "I'm sure you'll get enough stories out of him to last you through to your second marriages. Have fun now, ladies, and excuse me. Time to make a dollar."

Mary and Sara left Bob to his industry and went to sit on the corral.

The hot August morning was sleepy with the buzz of insects. A single scrap of a cloud backstroked across the river to the east, and overhead the sky deepened to a rich azure: a sky threatening heat. Scotch thistle and black-eyed daisies nodded in the tangle of pastureland, long since left to its own devices; sagebrush and drying grass swelled on the breeze. The frozen Rockies peeked over the western horizon. Sara pointed out the mirage to the south, the ghost town of Rosehip floating high in the air, the image shimmering with heat waves.

Suddenly, she straightened like a hooked fish and plummeted boots-first into the dust. From behind the fence, Tina giggled.

"Jesus, Tina. In High River that'll get you shot." Sara pulled herself back onto the fence and dusted off her pants legs. Then she smiled. "We figured you'd be tied up this morning."

"Nope. Not into that." Tina rubbed her eyes under a pair of aviator sunglasses and leaned up against the fence.

Sara pushed the glasses back up on her friend's nose. "Where'd you find those, your dad's top drawer?"

"No, I had more interesting drawers in mind."

"You're awfully quick this morning, my dear," Mary chimed in. "All right, enough small talk. Cough up the details now."

"Get your own."

"Shut up. Get up here and tell us everything." Sara reached under Tina's arm and helped her friend shimmy up on the corral.

From a distance, Darren looked at them and jerked his head toward his current interview — Phil, who laughed. The two men turned their backs and resumed their conversation.

Sara clucked at Mary. "You've got that man driven to distraction, you have."

Mary diverted the attention back to Tina. "Come on, out with it."

"Okay, let's see. After the two of you left — so suddenly, I might add — Chris hung around to square up the bar tab and the two rooms. Or at least that was his excuse. Turns out all he did was pay for that last round and leave Darren's contact information at work. I could be convinced to share that, by the way. At a premium, of course." She winked toward Mary.

Sara folded her arms and kicked her heels against the fence. "I'd say she'll get her own line on it soon enough."

"Will the two of you let me lead my own sex life, please?"

Tina smiled. "Of course, dear. Sorry. Now. Where was I? Yes, he squared up —"

"Is that a euphemism?"

Tina continued. "Bite me. And then, thoughtful woman that I am, I offered him a cup of tea. *Oops! All out at the bar.* So we went back to my place. Good thing I only live around the corner, eh? Doesn't leave them enough time to reconsider."

"My dear, what man in his right mind would?" Mary cooed.

Sara added, "Especially when he's loaded."

Tina gave her a sitting bodycheck and continued. "Anyway. He stayed. And it was nice."

Mary and Sara looked at each other. Mary spoke their shared thought. "It was nice? That's it?"

"Yeah. I'm pretty sure you're familiar with the mechanics. And this guy's, well, nice. I don't want to spoil it by talking about it."

"But that's how it *works*," Sara whined.

All three women jumped at the sound of Darren's voice. "How what works?"

Sara snapped at him. "Are we all operating on stealth this morning? Could you please stop that?"

Tina continued. "How it works is that when one of us beds a new —"

Mary hooked Tina's leg with her boot and pulled tight. "Darren, do you always barge into people's conversations unannounced?"

Darren scraped a freshie from his boot onto the bottom plank of the fence. "Imagine — real cowboys have real horses, full of real shit. But to answer your question, yes. I'm a reporter. It's my job."

Tina pushed her outrageous glasses up on her head and graciously changed the subject. "How are you feeling this morning, big spender?"

"Couldn't be better, really. The sun in the sky, charming company. A plum assignment. What more could a visiting newspaperman want?"

Mary shushed Sara as she began to speak. "We didn't get much of a chance to ask you about that last night," she said diplomatically. "What is it you're doing, exactly?"

"I'm here doing what the biz likes to call a colour piece for the paper: *Local Guys Brave Poetry*. It's a story with great tension. It's the artistic equivalent of a high-school dance: young poetic voices, gangly and untried, shuffling out nervously into the spotlight and potential humiliation. But they're brave, partly because they don't know any better, and partly because they're driven by the thrill of discovery. Or maybe just possibility. But similarly powerful. Don't you think?"

The question dangled rhetorically, and the reporter continued.

"Besides, there's a bit of a cowboy-poetry movement underfoot, and whether or not these guys realize it, they're part of it. It symbolizes what I see as millennial angst-driven, post-feminist social restructuring. A collective move to get in touch with the inner redneck, if you will."

Tina straightened her legs and admired her own muscles. She relaxed and ran her hands over the length of her thighs. "You run this past the *Voice* yet? Last time I saw them use the word 'feminist,' it was in the same sentence as 'meatballs'."

"Yeah. Unfortunately, they're interested in a slightly different angle: *Local Festival Wrangles Tourist Dollar*. But I certainly hope someone manufactures some tourists soon, otherwise Chris and I are going to be interviewing each other. Chris, as you know," he looked at Tina, "is shooting this for me. The editor doesn't normally pop for a photographer, but I convinced him to hire Chris freelance for this one. I think he could do a marvellous photo essay. And as long as the *Voice* gets their publicity shots, I figure Chris is free to get up to whatever else strikes his fancy." Sara elbowed Tina. Darren continued. "He really is brilliant. All he needs is a little step up."

"You don't strike me as an altruist," Mary teased.

"I'm not. But look at all the sympathy it's winning me with the locals," he said and wandered off again, toward two men pulling a set of risers out of the back of a horse trailer.

THE AFTERNOON PASSED IN HIGH COWBOY STYLE. THE poetry wasn't much to write home about: heroically rhyming couplets extolling the virtues of everything from the silence of the first morning star to watching the ball-game with a hidden mickey of 'shine; from watching a foal taking its first trusting steps to hanging the taxman by his silk tie from the highest jack pine; from the doldrums of the wedding bed to a son's last game of catch with his dad. It was all there, thrashing like a drowning swimmer. But it thrashed in living, breathing, screaming colour, and you had to admire it for that.

Men whose public speaking since grade school had been limited to *Strike! Ball!* and *Hurry! Sweep!* stood up in that corral, their buckles and snaps gleaming in the sun, and read their homemade poems from wrinkled pages, curled at the edges. Others recited them boldly from some attic in their brain reserved for just such an opportunity. Others still, whose voices normally filled the air around them with boorish chatter, sat mutely around the corral, their ears red with the thought of splitting open their personal lives like fish for so many crows. A few women stood up, but most people had chosen a rather narrow interpretation of "cowboy," and it wasn't until the women saw how truly bad some of their husbands' poetry was that they realized they should have shown them up. And that it wouldn't have taken much. *Next year*, they vowed. *Next year.*

Apart from the poetry, there were horseshoe tournaments and skeet-shooting competitions; truck-side stalls heaped with tooled leather belts, handmade rabbitskin moccasins, alfalfa honey, braided-wheat art, crocheted slippers and toilet-paper covers, dolls made of old woollen socks, hand-sawn lawn ornaments, and homemade fudge; and the unforgettable wood-smoked chili. Aside from a few cases of sunstroke and the odd pair of budding youngsters with inexplicably missing clothing, the afternoon went off without a hitch. Some tourists even showed up. Chris took pictures to prove it.

The day ended with a bonfire the size of a small star, as if all that poetry had roused in the men a collective hunger for light. Pick-up trucks materialized with hastily stacked heaps of split poplar; trailers appeared toting all manner of fire-worthy junk: broken school desks, splintered tables from the church basement, fence posts, the better part of a canoe, even the back wall of a double-seater outhouse, complete with the holes. Percy would find kitchen fixtures in the coals the next morning when he went to fire up a pot of coffee.

Darren and Mary had long since given up moving back their lawn chairs as the flames grew, and had retreated into the darkness with her moth-eaten Hudson's Bay blanket. They leaned against an old spruce stump, the top of which someone had hollowed out and filled with red geraniums;

the flowers were garish even in the amber light of a midnight fire.

"Do you think there are ants in this stump?" Mary asked, her head tipped backwards, face up at the moon.

"Why?" Darren asked, taking a swig from a flask.

"Well, it's either that, or my skin is prickling with the very closeness of you." She paused, and opened her eyes, doe-like. Then she snorted and choked, leaning forward in a heap of laughing and coughing.

"My dear, that's just the acid I slipped into your Budweiser." He thumped her back until she could breathe again.

Mary twisted and grabbed him by the wrist.

"Now you've got me." He gave her his best level gaze, his lips curling a dare. "So what are you going to do with me?"

Mary smiled slowly, and edged closer on the blanket. His eyes swam a little, and his breath was musky with whiskey.

She rose onto her knees, pivoted and straddled his lap. For starters.

## ❧ *Four*

THE FIRST FEW MONTHS WITH ROS WERE A DANGEROUS, difficult dance. Her wounds were still so fresh, her mind and soul so flattened from justifying and forgiving Charlie (the bastard who beat her) that the world beyond, with all its people and their needs and complications, defeated her. They were locked away in a sparkling glass cabinet without a key. But she so wanted to live. At her best, her eyes would glitter with hope and her breath would catch in her chest, her ribs a cage for a newborn heart. Then, like a child conditioned to fear what she can't control, she'd shrink from me, snapping and suspicious. The best I could do for her — for us — was to remain even and to listen. Unflappable.

Often this required forgiving things I couldn't. He'd beaten her. Held her down. She needed a vessel for all she couldn't bear but refused to forget. Every life begs recording and she'd been denied the right to tell. But I couldn't always be that person for her. I wanted Charlie punished. Truth be told, I wanted him dead.

I knew the best I could do for Ros was to help her start a new life, with a clean slate. But something in me wouldn't let that happen until I'd seen him, made sure somehow that he would stay where he was. One day I told Ros I had to go to Calgary to pick up a new fuel pump for the truck, packed a Thermos of coffee and took off south.

She'd shown me an early picture and I knew he worked in the university hospital as an orderly, so I figured I could find him. I stopped in at a florist near McMahon Stadium, picked up a bunch of daisies and went to the hospital. Roaming the halls posing as a lost visitor, I watched for Charlie.

I found him in the laundry room flirting with a girl half his age. He leaned over a counter with his face close to hers, his stare unwavering, with one foot balanced on its toe, wagging lazily back and forth. Her hands were planted confidently on either edge of the counter, her elbows locked in a way that suggested double joints, her young breasts pushed together in the deep "Y" that makes a lonely man weak in the knees. Twice her age or not, Charlie clearly wouldn't get out of this one unscathed.

I heard him say he was getting off at five, would she be interested in a drink? Her shift didn't end until seven, but she could meet him after that. He suggested Luigi's on Crowchild, ran his index finger from her elbow to the tip of her thumb and walked out. I ducked into the cafeteria.

I stood there with my wilting daisies, my heart thrashing in my chest, aware of the spectacle I was quickly becoming, blocking the double doors. I wanted to run back around the corner, take the girl's shoulders in my two hands and give her a shake. I wanted to show her Ros' purple welts, the way she flinched from me still when overcome by some phantom fear. But what could I do? Introduce myself as the obsessive new boyfriend and try to tell this young woman that I was really the one to trust? I put my urge aside and said a little prayer for the girl as I left on the second leg of my trip.

Luigi's was a lowbrow Italian dive in a strip mall just off the main highway. Beleaguered tea lights glowed shyly in smudged glass bowls. Piss-coloured light poured from grimy chandeliers and small square tables sulked under red-and-white plastic tablecloths. I sat at the end of the bar where I could watch the restaurant from the wall-size gilded mirror and ordered a cup of coffee.

Charlie came in around six wearing tight white pants and a navy satin cowboy shirt; he was attractive in the way train wrecks are. He sat at the bar and ordered bourbon, neat, with a beer chaser. He downed a couple of these and when conversation wore thin with the bartender, he turned to me. "Hey, buddy. Did you ever get them flowers into water?"

Blood rushed to my head.

"What?" I asked, my ears ringing.

"I saw you at the hospital today. A few times. You looked lost," he offered. The words he wasn't saying contorted his face into a sneer.

"No, man. I was just waiting to get in to see my wife. She was sleeping and the doctor said to come back."

"What kind of doctor wouldn't let a man in to see his wife? What's his name? I could have a word with him for you." He smiled lewdly — out of mockery or the nature of the word he wished to have on my behalf, I couldn't tell.

"Can I buy you a drink?" I ventured. "What is it you're drinking, Wild Turkey?"

"You're awfully observant. What's your name? I'm Charlie Kufeldt."

"Albert Smith," I said, offering my hand. He gave it one firm shake and held onto it just a little too long. *Albert Smith?*

Just then, the door squeaked open and in walked the laundry girl. Charlie stood up unsteadily to greet her. I bought him another drink and ordered myself a draft.

"Jackie," he cooed to her, holding open his arms. "My

little kitten." He smiled wryly, wrapped her in his long arms and nuzzled her neck. She threw back her head and was about to close her eyes when she noticed me.

"Jackie, I'd like you to meet just the nicest gosh-darned narcotics officer you'll ever meet. Mr. —" he stifled a chuckle, "— Albert Smith."

"Hello, Albert." Not understanding the humour, the girl gave me her hand and pursed her lips together in something that resembled a smile.

"I was just about to ask Mr. Smith to join us for a bite to eat." Both Jackie and I tensed. "You don't mind, do you, Jackie?"

"Charlie, I —"

"Oh, come on, Al. You're here by yourself and you've got a long drive home tonight."

I froze. "How do you figure that?"

He smiled. "Well, I just assume a man who chose to walk around the hospital for hours with wilting flowers while his wife slept must have nowhere better to be." He paused. "Am I right?"

I smiled thinly. "I suppose. But if you don't mind me saying so, Charlie, you look like you have other things on your mind besides kindness to strangers tonight."

I made to leave but he grabbed my arm. "Albert. Sit down." He tightened his grip and waved his other hand toward a booth. "Please."

Jackie's eyebrows squeezed together over her deep brown eyes, and only when the three of us sat down did Charlie let go of my arm. He called over a drink order for Jackie to the bartender, and the girl and I sat looking each other over like anxious lawyers.

My heart ached for the girl. She could melt in your mouth. Olive skin with a hint of rose over her cheeks and forehead. Healthy rounded body, with finely articulated hands like a musician's, her skin stretched perfectly to contain her. In her sheer blue floral dress, she was the breath of spring. She looked young, but carried herself as though she knew just what a man like Charlie was about. Maybe she could handle him. God knows the persuasion of a delicious woman.

"Jackie, how'd you wind up with Charlie here? Community service?"

She giggled.

"You should see this woman in a laundry outfit. Haunches like a greyhound." He scooped up her hand and squeezed it, too hard. She flinched and he threw her a kiss. With her other hand she scratched her hairline behind her right ear, growing pink with embarrassment or pain.

"Hey, Charlie. Let her go, man."

He dropped her hand like it had spiked in temperature by a thousand degrees and leaned back in his seat, turning his head toward me. "You know, Al, I've met your kind before. Best of intentions, Father Knows Best kind of thing. If you don't mind me saying, you know, if you don't mind a little truth, I'd say that you're lukewarm and judgmental. But Al, a lot of women like their men a little — I don't know. How would you say it, sweetheart?"

Jackie looked blankly at both of us and Charlie continued.

"Little Jackie is free to come and go as she pleases. But when she's with me, we do things my way." He wrapped his hand around her upper arm and slid her around the booth to sit beside him. He draped his arm over her shoulder. She rolled her eyes and kissed him on the neck.

I finished my beer and stood to leave. "It's really time for me to go," I said, the little hole in my stomach burning wider. "Interesting to meet you both." I put on my hat, offered Jackie my hand, and turned for the door.

"Say hi to all the good folks of Juniper Butte."

I stopped and turned around very slowly.

"I checked your wife's chart." He winked and pointed to my hat: Juniper Butte Esso.

THE LONG, DARK RIDE HOME WAS AN OLD FRIEND WHO needed no conversation, no explanation. The whispery moon hung high in the sky, its bright face tipped backwards in laughter or despair, and the Milky Way shone so coldly I thought it might be reflected in the fallow fields. The road spread out before me like a slumbering snake, hugging the hollows of the earth. I rolled down the window and let the cold black air run its fingers along my skin.

What did Charlie know? Had he tracked down Ros? Perhaps I had put her in danger by hunting him down. Maybe I'd ripped the maggoty corpse of her past from its deserving tomb. Would I tell her what I'd done? That he scared me as much as I'd imagined he might? That I could have said something to his next little snack, but didn't, in order to keep Ros safe? That it had killed me to leave the girl behind?

Blackness. Space. The comforting hum of tires.

Just then, a great horned owl swooped out of the ditch and twisted violently over the hood as it clipped the edge of the grille. My body bloomed with fear as I slammed on the brakes and veered for the shoulder of the road. My heart pounded. In a moment, when my knuckles loosened, I got out to see what I'd done.

The thing lay mangled and bleeding across the yellow line. Miles on either side, no headlights, acres of silence. I pulled out a set of work gloves from behind the seat and approached it slowly from the side, speaking softly.

The bird turned its head right around and stared at me with what I swear was pity. It blinked once and flinched when I reached to touch it. Its right claw was ripped nearly from its body and its wing twisted gruesomely in a confusion of bent and broken feathers.

I knelt down on the road and gathered the fallen bird in my arms. A massive thing, imposing and judicial, weighing no more than a kitten, its savage and protective heart faltering below paper skin. I took off one of my gloves and pulled it over its head. Then I wrung its neck.

ROS WAS TWO YEARS IN MY LIFE AND STILL EDGY AS A DOG AT the river afraid to swim. The day she found out she was pregnant, she came home early from school. She pushed through the screen door with a glass of iced tea in her hand and flopped out in the chaise lounge on the back patio. It was unseasonably hot — twenty-four degrees in May — and she'd changed into a little yellow skirt and had tied a denim shirt high up on her white belly. A flip-flop sandal dangled from a silver-tipped toe. I planted the shovel in the garden where I'd been digging potato hills and went over to sit beside her.

"Pipping off?" I teased, flicking off her sandals, slipping her feet between my thighs and running my hands up her smooth calves. "Not that I'm complaining, of course."

She said nothing for awhile; took a slurp of her iced tea, contemplating the glass. She swirled the ice with a delicate finger, then set it down on the fabric of her skirt.

She looked directly at me, extracted her feet and sat up, then leaned forward with her elbows on her knees, legs astride the chair.

"Look in my eyes and tell me, what do you see?" She opened them wide.

I paused, a man desperate for what was surely the one correct answer. "Uh, I see a woman of great intelligence, with extraordinary empathy, who —"

"Yeah, all right. Shut up." She paused. "I'm pregnant."

Another pause. I started smiling before I could speak. My heart swelled. "What?"

"I'm pregnant. I got the call this afternoon, over my third cup of coffee and two minutes before grade seven Language Arts. The secretary called from Dr. Cooper's office and said, 'Congratulations, would you like to schedule your first prenatal appointment?'"

I was still lost for words, my tongue swollen in my mouth.

"So I did," she continued. "Then I faked a headache and came home to tell you." She slurped again at her tea and settled back in her chair. She closed her eyes momentarily, then looked at me sideways and said, "Monday afternoon."

"Monday afternoon, what?" I asked, still stunned.

"That's my appointment. Are you available?"

"For what?"

She sighed, becoming administrative about the whole thing. "To come see the doctor. She wants to talk to you, too. See if you're fit for the job, tell you to treat me right, bring me breakfast in bed, that sort of thing."

I stared at her like some rare, precious thing — something totally foreign; something sharing my flesh. I took the glass out of her hand and held her close to me. It felt like the first embrace of my life. Then I held her at arm's length and looked her over. "How do you feel?"

"I'm not sure."

I gave her another hug and sat back again. "I mean, are you happy? Is this something you want?" I asked, my heart bursting with hope.

She cast her glance away. "I don't know."

A sinking feeling, like losing your grip on a person ready to fall. Her toes curled around themselves as she looked for the words. "I don't want to love it. Not yet." She paused again. "Please don't look at me like that. I don't want to love it until I know you will. Because if you don't want it, then I won't have it. And if I'm not going to have it, then it can't exist in my mind. Am I making any sense?"

I shook my head, then kissed her deeply, slowly, tasted the sugar on her tongue, tucked her unwilling curls behind her ears. "Excuse me now while I run out to stop traffic and tell everyone the news." I made to leave but she grabbed my hand.

"Randy." Her expression remained flat.

I waited. "What is it?"

"I just don't know if I'm strong enough to make it through."

"What are you talking about? You could wrestle bulls to

the ground with a broken arm. You could —"

"No," she interrupted. "Do you remember that time I cut my finger in the kitchen? It was a Sunday morning last summer. You'd just come home from a trip. We spent the morning out on the deck with tea. Remember?"

It was slowly coming back to me.

"Well remember how that cut bled and bled? I must have gone through half a roll of toilet paper trying to stop it. The Band-Aid was soaked the next morning, even."

"What? Ros —"

"It's okay. I didn't want you to know, because you'd make a big deal of it and take me to the doctor and I really can't be bothered with all that." She straightened up in her chair, smoothed down her shirt and looked out across the fence, avoiding my eyes.

"Anyway, it's something that runs in my family. We have flimsy veins. We're bleeders. My mom bled a lot during my birth, and it was probably only the fact that she went into labour on a shopping trip into the city that saved her. They had lots of blood on hand and when they got tired of that, they operated and clamped shut the veins around her uterus one by one until she finally stopped bleeding."

She stopped, then looked at me. "There's a real chance I might not make it through."

I was horrified. I held her close, then loosed my grip, afraid of hurting her.

"It's okay. I bleed. I don't break."

"Well, all right. We'll just make sure you're in Calgary a month before your due date. Or we'll hire you a personal obstetrician. Or better yet, a witch doctor. I don't know. Ros. *Have my baby.*" I stopped, the words electric on my lips. "Please."

She looked at me levelly, a blush rising to her cheek. She laid my hand on the tiny flat of her stomach. It was impossible to believe what was happening there.

"You're sure you want it?"

I nodded.

"Okay."

That decided it, and there was never another question.

FROM THE MOMENT THE WORDS WERE OUT OF HER MOUTH, my life changed absolutely and forever. I gave up my truck driving so I could be around more. Instead, I took odd jobs around town, clearing fields, shingling roofs. As the baby grew inside Ros, I came more and more to feel as though the two of them were my possessions and secret charge. I worried about the blood in Ros' veins. I was a traveller in a foreign market, drunk on the present and carefully dreading what lay beyond the next corner.

How had the world not stopped to watch her, how had it not collapsed with the weight of love?

We had arranged for Ros to stay with an aunt in Calgary

for the two weeks before her due date. I wanted her there earlier, but she resisted my worrying, said she had to get the house ready. And besides, she wanted to make the most of her last moments of solitude.

Her labour started one night as we lay together on the couch watching the late-night news on mute. She'd been out for a long walk that afternoon along the railroad tracks — a practice I disapproved of normally, let alone in the dead of winter when she was forty pounds front-heavy and a little short of breath — and had worked herself up nearly to exhaustion by the time she returned. She recovered in bed with plenty of sweet tea, but hours later she still seemed pale. We got her into some warm pyjamas and went out into the living room but soon after, a look came across her face that told me it had started. She struggled to stand while the water pooled at her feet. She was a month early.

I called Dr. Cooper, threw a few things in my old hockey bag and sped off to the local hospital. We would never make it to Calgary.

A little car approached and flicked its lights at me. I flipped to low beams and apologized out loud. Night was on full bore by now, the radio obnoxious. I turned it off, my ears singing in the darkness.

Her labour was short and uncomplicated, except for the tearing, to which the doctor quickly attended. Everything seemed fine. For being a month premature, the baby was robust and healthy, but she was spirited away to an incubator after only a few moments on her mother's chest. Ros lay there spent and sore with the baby on top of her and incapable of anything but love. She counted the baby's fingers and toes, and ran her fingers gently over the soft spot and over her red bum and in the folds behind her knee, and I stood there looking God in the eyes. I let the nurse lift the baby off her chest, believing Ros needed to rest. She held onto the baby's angry little fist for a moment, then her hand fell heavily to the side.

She was turning pale and when I looked down the length of her, blood was soaking through the sheets, a shadow lengthening. I stared dumbly, as if it were a puzzle with an elusive solution. The baby was gone away with the nurses, and the doctor was already on to new dramas. The blood spread with the momentum of floodwater.

The nurse returned and tapped me on the shoulder to ask if I wanted to see the nursery. Then she stepped around me to Ros and the rest of it passed, as if in a dream. I slunk into the corner as she lunged for the door and her mouth opened like a fish's mouth, pouring out silent words, tripping over themselves, children at a starting block. Two more nurses rounded the door with a bag of blood and a cart stacked with paddles and cords and needles, and they tipped the bed to lower Ros' head below her feet and found a vein, lazy with the lost blood, and called the doctor who ordered sutures and stitched her up quickly without freezing, neither of them flinching. Everything stopped as they waited, Ros' hand limp in the hand of a woman looking at the clock on the wall. Then, a lifetime or a second later, the doctor's hands on my shoulders and the words: *I'm sorry.*

At home, the house slept with its eyes open and the television whined a test pattern.

It was over.

## ❧ Five

THEY PULLED INTO THE DRIVEWAY IN DARREN'S RENTED CAR, heavily dusted from his weekend's many forays between town and the festival grounds. Bruce Springsteen snapped off in mid-sentence as the engine sighed to a stop. Mary giggling. Two doors slamming.

Randy stood up from the engine of his truck, slipped his wrench into his pocket and wiped his hands on a greasy rag. He squinted in the sun toward his daughter and the new thing she'd found.

Mary wrapped her arms around her father's waist and found the wrench in his pocket.

"What's this? Arming yourself already? You haven't even met him."

"I was just going at that timing belt."

"You've been saying that for the last thousand miles. Sometimes I think you just like to accessorize with tools. Which you're very good at, I must say. It's something I look for in men now. Pay attention, Darren. There will be a skill-testing question later. Randy, Darren. Darren, Randy." She twitched her open palm between the two men.

Darren stepped forward, his hands in the pockets of his jeans, his lean arms bent like wings. He wore a denim shirt, frayed where the arms had been ripped off, his snakeskin boots and copper-coloured mirrored sunglasses. To Randy, he looked more like a roadie or a pimp than the reporter he was rumoured to be. Juniper Butte was small enough that word of a newcomer in town still sounded like an alarm bell.

Randy nodded and waited for something more. "What's behind those glasses, Darren? And is your hand broken, or don't they teach you manners in journalism school?"

Mary cringed. Darren extended a hand.

"Dad, put your teeth back in your head. I've invited Darren over for supper. You guys want a beer?" Mary bounded up the steps without waiting for an answer, then returned with two Labatt's. She passed them over and smiled at her father.

"I'll let you two get to know each other." She closed the

door behind her and from inside came the muffled sound of the radio.

The two men looked at each other dumbly.

"Is this a test?" Darren finally asked.

Randy choked back a laugh and twisted open both bottles, then handed one to Darren. "What brings you out this way?" he asked, out of politeness.

"I'm doing a feature piece on the poetry festival for *The Western Voice*."

"Oh, that. Well, I suppose they're not hurting anybody anyway."

"It wasn't that bad, actually. I was surprised. Poetry is kind of like contortion: looks easy until you try it and someone breaks an arm. But they were pretty good. Must come from all that time under the big blue sky."

"Yeah, I guess." Randy smiled and sat down on the porch. Darren did the same.

"So I guess your job takes you some interesting places, then?" Randy ventured.

"Yup. Always good to keep a pair of sensible shoes handy. I guess that's what I like best about it."

"And the least?"

Darren smiled. "You writing a book?"

"Just making conversation. You don't like questions?"

"Guess not. I'm usually on the other end of them." He thought for a minute. "It's the deadlines I don't like.

Listening to people's stories all day. Trying to sort them out just enough to file a story for the next day. Wears a person out. Makes you feel like a bit of a gossip. I'd like to really get my teeth into something, you know?"

"Pays the bills doesn't it?"

"I suppose."

"Well, don't go getting too big for your britches. Know anything about engines?"

"Only enough to make me dangerous."

"Well, come here and tell me what you make of this timing belt."

When Mary re-emerged from the house, the two men were bent over the gaping mouth of Randy's truck, half-empty bottles of beer on the bumper and greasy smears on the backs of their thighs.

"Supper's ready!"

"What? You couldn't have been in there more than five minutes," Randy called from the inside the hood. He extracted himself and stood up smiling.

"Time stops for all things mechanic. I made vegetarian chili. It's amazing what you can do with a few dry goods and some ketchup. Must be the pioneer in me. Get in here, it's hot."

"A pioneer wouldn't be making vegetarian chili, I guarantee you that." Randy nudged Darren in the ribs and Mary smiled. The three went in for dinner.

"YOU DIDN'T TELL ME WHAT YOU LIKE BEST ABOUT YOUR JOB," Darren said to Randy, cleaning his plate with a heel of bread. Mary replaced his empty beer with a full one, brushing his shoulder as she did so.

The older man reached for a toothpick and pushed back from the table. "Oh, I don't know. I guess I just love the sound of the pavement under my wheels. People think it's the truck stops. That it's like being at the centre of your very own movie. Which I suppose is okay, if you're into tragedies. To me, there's nothing sadder than a room full of dislocated people who aren't happy until they're moving, then spend the whole time wishing they were home. And the food. Have you ever been given a reasonable serving in a Husky Big Stop? In fact, don't let it slip I just ate something without meat. They'll revoke my licence."

Darren grinned and took a pull of his beer.

"But I do love the driving. I love the movement. I love the feeling of moving faster than the world."

"Where do you go?" Darren asked, easing into an interview. "For a time, I had a route into Great Falls running dry goods. Usually something like fertilizer down and potato chips back, or sometimes bathtubs. Made no difference to me. My best gigs were pulling up with the truck to the warehouse, having some other poor grunt hook on a packed trailer, hand me the invoice, and wish me and Mary Godspeed."

Randy's face loosened as he spoke; he was happy to have

someone show some interest.

"Down into Calgary we'd go, where smog was thick as bad breath. Always came as a shock to me, no matter how many times I saw it. Always thought I was catching it on a bad day or something. That's the privilege of living in a small town, I suppose. Or one of them. Anyway, from Calgary it was south on the interstate where it seemed like the wind was always blowing. From every direction, at that. It'd yank the steering wheel right out of your hands, given half a chance." Randy demonstrated.

Mary smiled to see her father animated like this. They'd spent so much time together on the road, she'd forgotten how much he loved it.

"The damned wind. I mean, even the flags seem to get tired of it. The dogs sure do. Poor little buggers all hunker under some porch or other." Randy peered into the middle distance, redrawing his old route in his mind. "Down past Fort MacLeod the land starts getting different. Through the Blood Indian reserve, there's the sandstone cliffs and the rise of Cypress Hills on the horizon. All silent down there except for the hum of the tires and the wind. Anyway, we'd hightail it across the border, drop trailer, find a place to hole up for the night, grab a new trailer in the morning and get on back home."

"A giant diesel boomerang," Darren offered.

Randy laughed. "That's about the size of it. Now, none of

the places along the main highway stateside held much interest for us. Well, except for this one particular diner in Great Falls where you were expected to get your coffee your own damn self. Advertising a dislike for processed cheese in that establishment could win you a fistfight. You had to walk through the kitchen to get to the bathroom. Do you remember that place, Mary?"

Mary shook her head. "Nope."

Randy continued. "Anyway, most places along the main highway were little more than pit stops. But every chance we got, we'd take the long way down, past the mountain parks. Across the border there's a pretty alarming purple roadhouse with a billboard out front that reads *Turn left at the trees*. Kind of tells you what the land is like around those parts. But after that, the highway dips into the forest and then there's thirty miles of switchbacks. It's what a road would look like if it was blindfolded and spun around, if you know what I mean. Then: boom! Prairie scrubland, not worth a nickel. Horse country. Bombed-out car wrecks, trailers and white crosses on wires to mark the early passing of some carload or other."

Darren and Mary stole a glance at each other, enjoying Randy's elaborate description.

"We had a little place in Choteau where we liked to stay. That town was just plain honourable. The Roxy Theatre downtown with its free cups for the tobacco chewers and candy for a quarter. Red velvet curtains hanging like it was still 1952. The motel was easy to get into and out of in the truck, with a wide gravel pitch and a neon sign that could call you home for miles. Inside every room — and believe me, we'd had them all — was always an air conditioner sweating bullets, a plastic flyswatter and a little plastic basket with candies pinched from restaurants in Great Falls. Those candies turned Mary's tongue technicolour. You must remember that, Mary."

Mary nodded enthusiastically this time, though, truth be told, she couldn't quite.

"The restaurant down the street had a stack of coffee filters the size of kitchen sinks. Pie was served religiously at nine-thirty in the morning to a ring of farmers around the lunch counter. There was a thing called 'Traveller's Breakfast' on the menu that had fruit and yogurt, but by the cut of the hips on the cook, you knew to think twice before ordering it. The menagerie mounted on the wall — mountain goat, elk, some kind of speckled cat who'd seen better days — made Mary a little gun shy, but a stack of flapjacks and her own jug of syrup usually cured that."

Randy slowed down to a crawl. "It was earthly reward in the spring, with the beginning grass downy and green, the birds in the salt prairie ponds and a wind to tear salt from your eyes. Mary knew it too. 'Daddy,' she said to me once, 'There's so much I forget to remember.' " Randy leaned back again in his chair, lost somewhere in Montana.

Darren thought for a moment, looked at Mary, then back to Randy. "What would you say to me tagging along on a ride?"

"What?" Randy's forehead knitted. "What for?"

"I don't know. It'd make a great story, from what you just told me. I could come along as your road diarist. There's probably a whole book in it. Have you ever seen a book by a trucker? Or even *about* one, for that matter?"

Randy shrugged.

Darren continued, propelled by his idea. "I haven't. Kind of funny considering how opinionated your kind is, don't you think? Maybe it's because your hands are tied up all day. You can't write. Although driving across the prairies, you could probably make an exception."

"I suppose. Doesn't seem worthy of much ink, though."

"You'd be surprised. It'd be like the Old West, when reporters would tag along with posses on the hoof and wire back their stories." He smiled at Mary, who watched him with both dread and anticipation. "What do you say?"

Randy pondered a few moments, then shook his head slowly. "Free country, I suppose."

Mary nodded encouragingly. "It'll give you plenty of time to check him out, Dad."

Both men paused.

"Well, if you're serious," Randy began, "I was planning

to leave next week to take a load of potato chips into Oregon. Glamorous, isn't it?"

"Oh, shit." The words spit from Darren's mouth like cherry pits, and he instantly regretted them. He cursed the half-dozen beer in his gullet. Mary's face fell slightly.

"What's the problem?" Randy asked.

Darren rooted around for a handy excuse, sighed and slumped in his chair. He picked at his teeth for a second. "You want the truth?"

Mary shrugged. "I expect so."

"Okay. But you have to promise to listen until the end. Truth is, I have a criminal record. So it's difficult for me to cross the border."

Mary stared.

"Now, you promised you'd hear me out." Darren caught Mary's eyes, begged silently for her patience. "When I was about twenty, I had a girlfriend named Sandra. We didn't have a hundred bucks between us and I still didn't know what I wanted to do with my life. But it didn't seem to bother her and things were going really well. Then she got pregnant. Well, I freaked a bit, as you can imagine. For logistic reasons, mainly, like how was I going to feed the kid? But I got over it pretty soon. I even came to like the idea," he said, half congratulating himself, slurring his words only slightly.

"But then I guess the whole motherhood, protective thing kicked in with Sandra. And suddenly, she didn't find my free-wheeling lifestyle so attractive anymore. She met this rich accountant dude, who I guess she must have convinced to take pity on her, and in less than a month she was out of my bed and into his. Now, I would have come to accept that in time, I suppose. But he turned out to be a real bastard. Abusive and manipulative. And pretty soon, he started beating up on her. Word got back to me and I went around the bend. I tried to contact her, but I suppose she was feeling kind of foolish." He paused for a moment to choose his words, his eyes tracing the outline of the table.

"Then came the night I saw him in the bar with a sweet little redhead who was very much *un*-pregnant. I had a few drinks in me by this time and I got to thinking about what a sick, pathetic maggot he must be. So I went outside and waited for him. With the tire iron from the trunk of my car."

Mary blanched. Randy stared, unblinking.

"It's okay. He lived. But I spent a year in Drumheller for aggravated assault."

A full minute passed before anyone said anything.

Mary folded her arms across her chest. "What happened to Sandra?"

"She lost the baby. Then she took off north. To Yellowknife, I think. I haven't seen or heard from her since."

"And the accountant?"

"He's fine. Nothing a little plastic surgery couldn't take care of."

Randy pulled his upper lip into his mouth. Mary traced a fingernail along an invisible wrinkle in her jeans.

"Would someone say something, please?" Darren pleaded.

Mary's face contorted. "When were you planning on tell me about this little bombshell?"

"There's never exactly a *good* time, is there? Listen. It was a long time ago. It's not something I'm terribly proud of. Yeah, I overreacted. But you know what?" He turned to Randy. "There's not a man alive who hasn't considered doing the same thing."

Randy inspected his toothpick.

Mary stood up to go to the sink. She locked her hands at the edge of the counter and squinted through the window at two crows gabbing on the wire fence in the backyard. She shoved her hands through her hair then reached to fill the kettle with water. "Tea, anyone?"

"I think something a little stronger might be in order." Randy pivoted in his chair and grabbed a bottle of Alberta Springs from the cabinet. He uncapped it and poured a healthy shot into his and Darren's glasses. He wagged the bottle at Mary, who shook her head.

Randy took a good swallow of whiskey. When it had run through his every last capillary, he looked at Darren. "A man's not exactly comfortable when he hears his daughter's suitor is capable of braining someone in the dead of night, you know?"

"Oh, I know it. It's sent more than one conversation to the cleaners, you can be sure of that." Darren looked at Mary, who kept her back turned to the men. "Mary?"

No response.

"Mary. Please."

She turned to face him, her eyes lit with challenge.

"I know we haven't known each other long," Darren said carefully. "But you have to believe I would never hurt you." He downed his whiskey and shuddered slightly. "I think I should go."

"Just a minute." Randy gave Darren a level stare. "God knows I have done stupid things over a woman. And I'm prepared to believe that a man can change. But I want you to know, son, that *any* man who mistreats my daughter will come to regret it. Do I make myself clear?"

Darren returned the look, nodded.

"Okay. Goodbye to you then, and maybe we'll see you again sometime." Randy batted his tumbler back and forth between his fingers.

Darren stood, briefly laid his hand on Mary's arm and grabbed his keys.

Outside, he let out the air from his lungs like a whale lumbering toward the sky.

## ❧ *Six*

WHEN PEOPLE DIE, THEY KEEP THEIR SEAT AT THE TABLE. I suppose that's why there was never anyone for me after Ros. Every time I sat down, there she was, green eyes gleaming, elbows akimbo, and smooth skin stretched tight over the bones of her chest. Mary never even saw her mother, except in those first few moments of screaming fluorescence, and I suppose she must have wondered when she was growing up why her daddy would sometimes sit and stare away the night. Mary never knew her mother, but there she was — Ros glowing hotly in Mary's own two eyes. And despite her stray dog for a father, Mary managed to grow up a lady.

I asked Ros for help many a time. How do I quiet the girl, cool her fever? A mother would know these things, I thought, like the blood in her veins. But Ros was useless as a saint. All she could ever do was beam goodwill, and leave the sleepless struggle to me. And I'd be damned if I was going to give over my Mary to one of her aunts. They could raise kids easily as pumpkins, but I decided early on that if my girl had any of her mother in her at all, she'd rather trip along foolishly with me than squeeze into some pre-cut life. So that's what we did. We stumbled, we struggled, but we grew to understand one another.

I raised my little girl the best way I knew how, which, it turned out, was like a boy. What would you expect? I certainly wasn't going to be strapped with a housebound ninny, and seeing as how we were in for the long haul, I at least wanted her to be decent company. As soon as she was old enough to sit up on her own, I dug the rig out of the mothballs and got us back on the road. The pull of the road was like one long, easy slide downhill. Mary loved it. She drank in the world like she might never get another chance — wanting it, coveting it. It put the wanderlust in her early. Taught her the value of seeing things with open eyes.

My regular gig was hauling up produce from Penticton, which held a certain allure: all that sweetness, fresh and fragile, a race against decay under the dusty sun. It meant we were in Golden once every ten days or so, and the girls at the Two Table Café loved little Mary. Doted on her like she was one of their own.

"Mary, Princess. Will you be having tea this morning with your egg and toast?" I remember Ruby wiggling her pencil over her order pad and bearing down on the girl with fiercely sparkling eyes. At nine-thirty, the breakfast run was chugging to a stall, and Ruby's stockings slumped in exhausted folds around the top of her white loafers. She was a grandmother. She looked about forty.

"Yes."

"Yes, what, dear? Is your Daddy teaching you no manners at all?"

"Yes. Please," Mary said politely, though even at the ripe old age of three, she did not appreciate being patronized.

"I'll have the usual, Rube." I told her. "And do us up a loaf of homemade bread for the trip, will you?"

"You got it." Ruby marched to the kitchen, then promptly returned with a basket and hauled up a chair.

"You want some crayons, Princess?" she asked, offering Mary her stash of chewed and broken nubs of wax.

"Yes, please," she said, helping herself to the works, and smoothing over the back of the place mat and a little frill of water where the glass had sat.

I remember how the girl cocked her head to the side. Her left foot snaked thoughtfully behind her right, up high in her chair, flecks of pink paint on the nails of her miniature dusty toes. With a yank on her halter top, she began to draw. One round face with crooked eyes and an unruly mop of yellow hair: me. A smaller figure with equally unruly hair and a blue triangle for a dress. Then a pause. She looked up and searched my face, then looked at Ruby. Then she set down the crayon, hopped out of her chair and ran out of the dining room, hooked a left down the hall and away toward the bathroom. I looked at the pair of figures she'd drawn, but for an instant saw only the one missing, the absence settling in my stomach like poison. Ruby looked at my sheet-white face and went out for our tea. A few minutes later, Mary rounded the corner again and marched up to our table, wiping her hands on the bum of her patched jeans. She climbed back up in her chair and reached for her warm mug, more milk than tea.

I smoothed her hair, half-stood from my chair, and kissed her on the forehead like a blessing. Like a prayer.

Ruby took the basket of crayons and trundled toward the kitchen for our breakfast. We ate wordlessly while humming along to our own country music soundtrack.

Alone, together.

SEEING THE WORLD THROUGH MARY'S EYES MADE ME A gentler person, simpler. Young children don't understand nuance. To them, things are good, or things are bad: surgical reason. And there's some value to that. For a typical thirty-two-year-old guy, raising a kid on your own was *bad*. But Mary prevented me from doing certain things, being certain ways. When she was born, I was a young man with ideas, ambition. A thirst for a beer or six when the mood struck me. Raising a child alone — and a girl at that, foreign creatures that they were — meant I was home in bed at ten more nights than I would have liked. It saddled me in some ways. But what was I missing, really? A lot of dark, dusty nights with women on my mind, forgetting myself. Ros was gone, and she was all the woman I seemed to need. She filled me in life, and haunted me in death — there was nothing left of me to want or be wanted. I ate, slept, and dreamt, all for the love of Mary.

Having Mary discover the world for the first time in my truck was a privilege. It taught me what an innocent mind notices, showed me patterns of things already beaten out of my worn-out mind.

"Daddy, why do things closer up move faster?"

"What, Angel?" The dreaded question, *Why?* "Oh. Uh, it's not that they move faster. We're the ones moving." Why was there no section on physics in any of the parenting manuals? "The trees look like they're zooming away compared to the mountains in the distance because they're closer. It's like a giant walking past an ant compared to a giant walking past an elephant. Get it?"

She looked out the window to contemplate her new knowledge. I prayed she wouldn't repeat this to anyone with more than two years of formal education. It's the saving grace of parents that people will believe anything said with authority.

Mary rolled down her window and tried to hang her hand from the top of the window frame like me. She found she was too short and when she crawled up on the door, I pulled her back down into her seat.

"Seat belt, little lady. You'll get sucked out like a puff of smoke." She made a face but obliged.

"Why do things close up sing higher?"

"Sing?" I looked at her. She was pressed up against the door, pleased with herself.

"Yeah, listen."

I turned off the radio. A high fence loomed alongside the road. As we passed, it whined like wind through a lonely house. And when it fell behind, the sound of the motor dropped away to a deeper, mechanical moan.

"See?"

"That, my dear, is because sound is like water. It travels in waves. And when they hit the fence, they bounce back and make ripples, which everyone knows are much more gossipy than big breakers. So they're higher-pitched. Whiny, like." I looked at her out of the corner of my eyes, laying down the bullshit thicker than on a slaughterhouse floor. Like I said, blame it on the manuals.

Other kids might have gone snaky cooped up in that

cab, with the endless drone of radio and squelch on the CB, the motor humming through our bones. But I bought her some paints to give her something to do — eight colours in little plastic pots with hinged plastic lids attached on stiff arms of plastic like molecular bonds in a chemistry set, and a little brush with fine, tapered bristles. She loved those paints. She was careful to keep her hues separate, to wash her brush in a little sawed-off Coke can of water. She'd paint through a whole scrapbook, then when that was finished, she'd start on newspapers and gas receipts, our little gift to the Tax Man. And not your ordinary preschool landscapes and domestic scenes, either. No, Mary's concoctions were always what you'd call abstract, I suppose. Shapes and colours mixed up in a kind of painterly alphabet soup. Repeating patterns. Lines begun on one sheet, continued on another. Once, she insisted on painting her window, covering it with a patchwork of repeating stars that split the sun like cathedral glass.

And she learned all the songs in my meagre eight-track collection. She so loved the Eagles that I had a little shirt made up for her in brown velveteen letters: "Flat-bed Girl." She wore it threadbare, and cried when I finally told her she'd grown out of it. The thing still hangs on her bedroom wall, above her high school diploma and a framed picture of her mother in fake pigtails and a Stetson. She'd fall asleep in Revelstoke and wake up in Lake Louise, bathed in the warm glow of dashboard lights, whining about what she'd missed.

At night we'd pull off some place along the highway and make up the bed in the cab. I'd zip her into her pink footed pyjamas, roll her into her nylon sleeping bag, tuck Jeremy the Elephant under her arm, kiss her on the forehead and settle under a quilt Ros had made especially for my road trips.

"Dear God. Please forgive me for saying that lady at lunch today was fat. Please let my fish be alive when I get home, and please let that be before *Disney*. Please bless Daddy, Auntie Margaret and Auntie Brenda. And please say hi to Mommy. Amen."

She'd roll over onto her side and crane her head back to watch the stars over the swaying trees, or the northern lights, if we were lucky. Her eyes would grow heavy, her breaths deep. Warm, sweet breaths. Baby breaths. I'd lay awake a long time, full of her fragility. This life that Ros and I created. I'd relax the muscles in my back, let the tension bleed into my shoulders, my arms. Clench my hands into tight fists, then let them go.

My little girl, my little bird.

# ✤ *Seven*

QUITE SOME TIME PASSED BEFORE MARY FELT COMFORTABLE talking about Darren with her father. But when they finally broke the ice, both seemed to have come to accept Darren's past, much as one accepts a lame dog. A few weeks, a few long distance phone calls and some beautifully crafted letters later, Mary had set aside the unfortunate dinner conversation and was nearly as enamoured of Darren as before. She believed that with the exception of one regrettable mistake, he was a tender person. In fact, if you disregarded the cold-blooded ambush thing, the fact he'd risk his own future to protect a woman he loved seemed admirable in an unsettling kind of way. And Randy, after some soul-searching, had actually come to believe what he told Darren that night at supper. He did believe in the possibility of redemption, and his own shame regarding a certain botched tryst — one that had happened more than five years ago, and that Mary, luckily, never knew anything about — served as a cautionary tale: flesh can render one temporarily insane.

Around this time, Mary brought up the topic of her tenure at her father's house.

"Dad," she announced over breakfast one day, "what would you think about me moving out?"

"What?" Randy set down his coffee and looked hurt. "What for?"

"What for? I'm twenty-one years old. Don't you think it's time?"

"Well, there's no schedule for these things, as far as I know. Don't you like it here? Do you want to paint your room?"

"No, Dad. It's not about paint. I've been staring at the same ceiling since before I was potty-trained. It's just time for a change of scenery."

Randy pushed away from the table. "Am I cramping your style or something? I thought I gave you plenty of room to come and go."

"You do, Dad. This isn't about you, as they say. It's just, you know. Time." She paused. "I mean, if that's okay. What do you think?"

"Where were you planning on going?"

"I don't know. I don't have a *plan* or anything. It's just an idea right now."

Randy rested his chin on his hand, and looked out the window. It was hot already at nine o'clock. He watched the air above the cab of his truck ripple. Even the birds had lost the heart to sing.

"I've had you to myself for a long time."

"Yeah. Time to spread the wealth, eh?"

He managed a weary smile. "I guess I should have known this was going to come sometime." He rubbed at the stubble on his chin.

"It's not like I'm leaving the country, Dad. Maybe I'll just go downtown or something, eh?" She stepped toward him and laid two hands on his shoulders, then touched her forehead to his.

"It's just—the thought of the house without you," he swallowed, "makes me something very near afraid. Makes room for all those other absences you know? There'll be all those little bit of pieces of you waiting around to ambush me."

"Lost mittens under the deep-freeze. Wishbones putrefying in the china cabinet. That sort of thing."

"Well, maybe your old man's getting sentimental in his old age. Give me a break. No one wants to be lonely."

"You'll never be lonely, Dad. I won't stand for it." Mary kissed him on the forehead, and took her tea out to her easel.

THE STRANGEST THING ABOUT THE RING OF THE DOORBELL a few days later was that it happened at all. Only salesmen, cops and missionaries rang the doorbell in Juniper Butte. Still in her pyjamas, Mary got up from her newspaper and went to the door.

"Darren?" She scratched her arm and ran a hand through her hair. "It's Wednesday. What are you doing here?"

"I wanted to see you."

"It couldn't wait until I was dressed?"

"Since when has that mattered?" He scooped her into a ravenous bear hug. She returned his hug impatiently and tugged him through the front door.

"Where's your father?"

"Out in the back, bonding with his rig."

"Good, we have plenty of time then." He picked her up and started for the bedroom.

She wiggled free and smoothed out her clothes. "I'm flattered, Darren. But really. What are you doing here?" Her thick hair stood up on its ends around her face. In her threadbare powder blue pyjamas, she looked like a kid carried in from the car after a sleepy road trip. He stood back to admire her.

"What?" She wrapped her arms around her middle defensively.

"Nothing." He smiled and sat back in the squeaky recliner. "I'm here to start a new life." He fumbled in his coat pocket for his cigarettes. He flashed his lighter toward her. "Mind if I smoke?"

"I don't, but Dad does."

Darren considered this a moment, put the smokes back in his pocket and smoothed his hair with two hands. A truck grumbled by on the road outside, sending a terrier in the neighbour's yard into fits.

"Let's just call it a new chapter. When one door closes — " he said with an ironic twist of the head.

"Would you please stop talking in riddles and tell me what you're on about?"

"I got fired. And since it was all your fault, I figured you owed me."

"What do you mean, you got fired?" Mary slumped against the couch, deflated. "You're the best reporter they have."

He shrugged and crossed his legs. One foot bounced like a kid on a trampoline. "The best one they *had,* maybe."

"What did you do? And what the hell does any of it have to do with me?"

"I erred in aspiring to the greatness you inspired," he said with a flick of the hand. "You helped me see the poetry in the poetry. The meta-poetry, if you will. And that's what I wrote. My boss Kitchener was expecting The Farm Report with pictures. And instead of doing the sensible thing and claiming my mastery as his own, he got scared. Scared of it, scared of me. Kitchener is a slob. He's a sloppy thinker who lacks the ambition to see beyond his next deep-fried meal. I'm in a different league altogether," Darren was unafraid of admitting, "and that's intimidated him from the get-go." He looked past her and around the room. Last time he was here, he hadn't really paid attention.

A long, unframed canvas hung over the doorway to the kitchen, fairly dripping with silver. A long 'V' fanned from right to left, and seemed to emerge from two silver depressions cupping two black comb-like things. He squinted and pulled slightly sideways, as though the meaning of the image would expose itself like a schoolyard pervert if he turned his back. Then he saw it: the back two feet of a water skimmer, caught in forward motion. The paint strokes were nearly digital in definition.

On the west wall, above a ratty loveseat covered by a patchwork quilt, was a smaller square painting. This one looked to be smeared together with a butter knife: a nod to the melodrama of the Group of Seven, maybe. The central image was a pine, twisted with age and rot, and black against a reddening sky and furrowed earth. Surrounding this was a square of black just inside the edge of the canvas, which gave the viewer the impression of looking out through a window, or that the edges were slowly squeezing the world from view. Next to that was a painting of a blackbird and a fence post, and some words he couldn't quite make out from this distance.

In the corner she'd pinned a photo he recognized by Courtney Milne, of a sand dune carved into the shape of rather fetching female loins, complete with a hollow for a navel. Mary's nearly finished impression of it sat on the nearby easel. The sky was blood red at the apex and bled to the colour of straw at the horizon. A tiny man wearing a derby and pin-striped suit was busy tattooing a set of footprints across the dune's upper left thigh as he approached the hollow, which was pierced with a single banyan tree. She'd just begun work on the shadow.

She was good.

He looked out the window and exhaled deliberately through pursed lips. "Well, are you happy to see me or not?"

Mary pried herself from the couch and padded over to sit in his lap. She buried her index finger in the hair at the back of his neck, traced it around wordlessly, then pulled his face close to hers.

He smiled as she kissed him.

"SO, DARREN, RUMOUR HAS IT YOU'VE COME TO STAY FOR awhile." Tina was rubbing down the counter at the bar, which plainly needed no further cleaning.

"That's right," he said and buried his fingers further into Mary's back pocket. "I'm here to become Juniper Butte's model citizen."

"I see. And we have the poetry festival to thank for this?

From the time in grade twelve when I read that crackhead poet going on about caves and domes and Olivia Newton-John songs I knew poetry was a bad scene. 'In Xanadu did Kubla Kahn ...' What the hell is that? Never touch it myself."

Mary shot her friend a mild warning, then suggested to Darren they move to a table. They chose the corner of the bar underneath the television and the stuffed jackfish, and sat down across the table from one another, Mary with her elbows out like a mantis, and Darren tilted back appraisingly in his chair: his favourite position.

"So, you're not sorry at all about leaving the *Voice*?" she asked.

"It's okay, you can call it for what it is. I got *fired*. And no, I'm not sorry. I got out with my soul intact, which is more than I can say for old Oscar Meyer."

"Who?"

"Kitchener. My boss. He reminds me of meat by-product the way his gut sags toward the floor and his legs puff out around the tops of his socks, especially after —"

"Okay, stop. I get it."

"Frankly, I was starting to find his ass-rag of a paper a little oppressive. How about you ask me what I'm going to do now?"

Mary shrugged in acquiescence.

"What I really want to do is write for the big magazines. Get a few good commissions per year, do some travelling, slide some work Chris' way, and sit back and really think about the big picture. I never got the chance to do that when I was turning around copy for people who were more interested in the weekly Co-op inserts than the news. I didn't fit in at the *Voice*. Kitchener knew it; I knew it. Firing me was the best possible solution. Anyway, I have no excuse now. I filed for pogey on the way up here. That should give me a fair few weeks to get some contacts and some money rolling in."

Darren stopped and looked at her. "And a fair few weeks to get to know my Mary better. Come here." He pulled a chair around the corner of the table and held open his left arm. She got up and sat down in the chair beside him. He scraped it closer and dropped his arm around her, folding his fingers over her shoulder.

He dropped one hand and deftly lit a smoke. They sat for a few moments in comfortable silence as he took a few drags; then he crushed the cigarette.

"What'd you do that for?"

"The first few puffs are always the best. The rest is just habit."

She raised her eyebrows and poked him in the side.

"Not to worry, my dear." He bent down and traced his tongue from the corner of her mouth, down under the curve of her jaw. She smiled broadly as her toes went numb.

"Rent a room, why don't you?" Tina hollered out from

behind the bar. She pitched a wet rag across the room, which landed short and slid across the floor to rest at Darren's foot.

"Fine idea," he said to Mary.

He led her out of the bar to his Camaro, chucking the rag over his shoulder at Tina on their way out. They drove to the cemetery and had quick, cramped sex under a moth-eaten army surplus blanket in the back seat.

LATER THAT NIGHT, AS DARREN LAY ON RANDY'S COUCH LIS-tening to the house settle around him, he buried his hands in his hair and exhaled, sinking deeply into the well-worn cushions. He shifted slightly, to relieve the pressure already building up in his lower back from the bowing of the springs, and looked again around the room.

The paintings were completely different creatures in the light of the street through the darkened windows. Shadows. Like faces you can't quite make out. Haunting. Imperious. He rolled the other way to face the back of the couch, which screeched in protest.

A deep tectonic motion was beginning somewhere in the quick of him. His stomach felt weak, his throat dry. He couldn't seem to close his eyes. His mind waged battle with the night.

He reminded himself this could be good. Mary was the first warmth of sun on a spring morning, the release in a full-body stretch. Yet she was gritty, too. She could handle a person like him without too much shock and upset. But the truth was, he didn't have a great record at this kind of thing. He would start out wanting to be loyal and loving. Then, as if a free pass to polite society had expired, he'd change. Or *they* would change, he could never be sure. After a time, women just started to expect things. Their need would become a smouldering coal, quietly burning all the oxygen in the room until the people inside just went to their sleep. Or someone smashed the window. And this was the role for which he was particularly well-suited: Darren the Liberator.

Each and every time he tried a relationship, he began with hope and ended in an insoluble knot of frustration.

Then there was this thing between Mary and her father. They seemed hermetically sealed. How could another person ever slip in there? Randy would not be simply handing over his daughter to anyone. In fact, he was bound to make life hell for anyone who even wanted visiting rights.

And just what was he, Darren, doing here anyway? Out of work in a small town with ... what was it Kitchener accused him of? Delusions of competence. Believing himself destined for greater things. How original.

He rolled over on his back and stared at the ceiling. Two hot tears pooled in the corners of his eyes and slipped down into his hairline. He took a few breaths to collect himself.

That Tina was one hot-looking woman. Something

about bartenders — particularly stacked ones — had burrowed its way under his skin. Darren figured she would know what to do around a bedframe. The other one, Sara, was too mouthy. Always explaining things. Probably never get her to shut up long enough to —

He caught himself. This was going to take some serious cross-training.

He would remember that Mary was a beautiful girl, just beginning herself. He would remember that her father probably hadn't had the easiest go of the last two decades. He would remember that he was not very good at all this and he would attempt humility. All that stuff they had made him rattle off to get parole. Maybe it wouldn't be so bad to come to believe it.

The crust was beginning to move again. His throat tightened. His lungs forgot themselves. Then, out of nowhere, a sob erupted into the air around him. He jammed a fist in his mouth, and in the moments after the sob passed, he heard the floor creak in the old man's bedroom. Eventually, in the silence, he fell into a fitful sleep.

## ❧ *Eight*

ALL THINGS CONSIDERED, I MADE OUT OKAY AS A SINGLE, blundering father when Mary was little and really no different from a boy. But inevitably she began to grow up, and I met the signs with a mixture of pride and dread.

For thirteen happy years, Mary was aware of her own body only insofar as it was the thing that got her around in the world. Sometimes she had to feed it and sometimes it let her down and needed a little fixing. But mostly it bent and ran and stretched and did everything a regular kid could ask for.

But then a curious thing started happening. Her shirts wouldn't lie flat against her chest anymore and she began to be self-conscious. She refused to let me in the bathroom when she was taking a bath.

I wanted to face this one about as much as I wanted to enrol in advanced calculus by correspondence.

Fortunately, my sister Brenda had the wherewithal to see me through it. One Saturday, she whisked Mary off to Red Deer. She dropped Mary off at ten o'clock that night with an A&W root-beer glass and a crackling plastic bag from The Bay.

"Hold on," I called out from the living room as she rounded the bottom of the staircase and started upstairs. "Did you have a good time?"

"Yup. We went to a movie. Then we went for a hamburger, and I got to keep the glass, see?"

"Looks like you went shopping, too. What'd you buy?"

She flushed a brilliant fuschia.

"Stuff," she said quickly, then ran up the stairs and slammed the door behind her.

I didn't see her again until breakfast, when she came down in an ironed pink shirt. Something about her looked strange, but I couldn't put my finger on it. It wasn't until I helped her on with her coat, and my hand brushed against the back of her shirt, that I figured it out — a bra strap. I sent her out the door without saying a word, then called Brenda to ask her what I should do next.

"Say nothing. Do nothing. You're welcome, by the way.

That girl would have been twenty-two before she knew what was happening to her, had she been left to her daddy's care."

"Thank you. I just ... You know."

"I know. She'll probably be getting her period within the year, in case it hadn't occurred to you."

"Oh, it's occurred to me, all right."

"Don't worry, we've got her all stocked up now. If she ever wants to stay home from school one morning for no apparent reason, call me. Or if you see blood in —"

"All right, I get the picture."

"Big tough man, eh, Randy? You've got a young woman on your hands. You'd better come to accept that. Now are the two of you coming over for dinner Sunday night?"

I don't know when Mary came of age, exactly — thank God for sisters and small mercies — but things changed between us after that. She wasn't as eager to come with me on trips, and was hungrier for the company of other girls. She started using her allowance to buy magazines that catered to the over-sexed or brain-damaged, or both. She spent inordinate amounts of time on the phone.

I would have been worried, had she not also been getting more and more adept at the easel. I encouraged her by keeping her supplied with paper and brushes. And as she showed no signs of giving it up — in fact, her vision seemed to be getting more coherent and sophisticated — I started bringing home scraps of wood and canvas which I fashioned into passable canvas stretchers. Her painting gave us something to have in common.

And by the time she turned sixteen, it was time for her to hit the road again, this time on her own terms. The day after her birthday, she aced her driving test — of course — and got her licence. By the time we got home, Brenda had parked in the front driveway the aging red hatchback I'd bought off a guy in Stettler. Mary's delivery to womanhood was complete. She had a passion, and a means to achieve it.

And someone to watch over her, whether she wanted it or not.

THERE'S A NIGHT IN MY LIFE THAT I'M NOT TERRIBLY PROUD of. And I'll tell it to you, because it's how I know a man can do stupid things in the name of flesh.

Maybe it was sixteen years alone, or maybe it was just me resisting the state of suspended animation that the time between winter and spring tends to bring on. Probably it was the approaching anniversary of Ros' death. But whatever it was, something came over me. "Those old tomcat feelings," as Tom Waits puts it. Anyway, I needed to put on a fresh shirt and get out of the house.

Late one Saturday afternoon, when Mary was old enough to fend for herself, I scrubbed myself up, zipped myself into a respectable pair of jeans, and jumped in the truck, bound for Calgary. I cranked up the heat and rolled down the window, letting the cold wind spill over my face and through my hair. The sun was lazy on the horizon, as if it couldn't muster up the energy to make it any higher. Snowbanks clung impossibly to silvered snow fences along the ditches, threatening to collapse into themselves and the greedy fingers of gravity. A snowy owl blinked from the top of a power pole. A horse stood statue-still in a blanket in an empty corral waiting for spring. Heat waves shivered from the dashboard, and when I looked out from the corner of my eye, the landscape swam. It was good to be here, good to be alive; it's funny how much passes when you're not looking.

It was nearly six o'clock when I pulled past city limits, which lately seemed to be opening like a ravenous mouth. Time for supper. Or an early movie at the drive-in, if I hoofed it. I picked up a burger and onion rings on the way.

There was a duster double-header showing on screen five, and hardly a car in the lot. No one appreciates westerns anymore. Off to my left sat an ancient couple in a dusty blue Lincoln Continental. To my right, a fat man with thick glasses was simultaneously smoking a cigarette and hooking up the stereo in his rusty black Tercel. I ran the black speaker chord through my window, then set off for something to drink.

The canteen was run by a youngish woman with jet black hair wearing a blue sweater and jean jacket. The collar of a pink cowboy shirt peeked up underneath and snagged her long beaded earrings as she turned her head this way and that. I watched her as the short line stuttered forward.

"What can I get you?"

I ordered a root beer, and continued gawking while she scooped the ice into a cup and opened a bottle of Dad's. Instantly smitten, I rooted in my pocket for change, then wandered back to the truck.

*The Ballad of Gregorio Cortez* staggered like a horse thief as I fought to pay attention to the screen: horses glistening black against a western sky, dust lingering like frightened children, big country that any man — good or bad — could get lost in, and poor, misunderstood Gregorio, who knew right from wrong, but ran, like any man would. Poor Gregorio, who knew that a good horse is better than a coal fire any day.

*Run, Gregorio, run.*

I finished my root beer. I tried to recall if the woman in the canteen had a wedding ring, but couldn't.

"Thirsty guy," she said, handing me another root beer during the intermission. She smiled, and nodded me off to the side while she served the few people remaining in line. Two cups of cocoa for my friends from the Lincoln, a bottle of Orange Crush for a woman in a black sweater who was clearly humouring someone, a hot dog for some pimply kid's girlfriend.

No sign of a wedding ring. The night was looking up.

"What's your name?" she asked, picking up her hair in one hand and letting it spill down her shoulders. She was beautiful, in spite of the unforgiving light from the fluorescent bulbs.

"Randy Thompson: Country Boy In for a Night on the Town."

"From?"

"Juniper Butte."

"I see. They don't have movie theatres up in Juniper Butte?" She smiled as she said this, which made it forgivable.

"Nope. And you know? There's just nothing like sitting in an idling car straining to hear the movie over the screaming of the heater fan. I think the carbon monoxide aids in the suspension of disbelief. What's yours?"

"My disbelief?"

"No, your name."

"Helen."

I waited for her to continue. "That's it?"

"That's it for now."

"Do I get more later?"

"Maybe." She smiled again. I went back to the truck and waited for the movie to end.

I SLAPPED DOWN A TEN SPOT FOR TWO PINTS OF HARP AND carried them back to the table in the corner. Helen had taken off her sweater, and her sleeveless cowboy shirt was unsnapped dangerously low. The shadow from her chin disappeared between her breasts, and I did my best not to follow where it went. Her arms were long and thin, and small shadows fell in the hollows between her bone and sinew. I passed her a beer, and we chinked glasses. My wallet was uncomfortable in my back pocket, so I plucked it out and threw it on the table.

"So, do you make a habit of picking up movie concession-stand workers on your outings to the big city?"

"Is this a job interview?"

"No, but I like to screen men before I let them pick me up."

"Too late for that, isn't it?"

"I suppose so. But go on. Humour me. It might heighten my anticipation."

"Well, let's see. I'm excellent at staying awake for long periods of time."

"Let me guess. You're a doctor."

"Nope."

"A student."

"Of some things."

"A truck driver."

"Right! You'd make a great charades partner."

"Why, thank you. What do you drive?"

"Produce, mostly. Odds and ends in the winter. Feed. Shingles. What are you good at?"

"I'm good at slinging root beers for strangers. I'm good at making homemade key lime pie. I'm exceptional at guessing what colour paint will be when it dries. And I'm an uncanny judge of character."

"I see. And what kind of character am I?"

"Good enough to hang out with me."

I choked. A wet laugh somersaulted through the air. "Helen, I have to tell you, I haven't done this in a long time," I said, with emphasis on the 'long.'

"Not many women in Juniper Butte, eh?"

"Something like that."

"Ever been married?"

"Yeah."

"And?"

"Ros died having our daughter."

"Oh. Sorry." Helen searched my face for signs of what to say next. "What's your daughter's name?"

"Mary," I said, brightening. "It's her sixteenth birthday pretty soon."

"She'll be driving soon, just like her dad."

"Yeah," I chuckled. "I suppose you're right. Hard to believe."

I fiddled with my glass. Slowly, Helen waded into the uncomfortable silence. "Want to hear a story?"

I leaned back in my chair and let go a lungful of air. "Okay."

"It ain't pretty."

"Neither am I. Fire away." I tried to smile encouragingly. I was going to have to shake this head of mine if I was going to show this lady a good time.

"My daddy disappeared when I was a little girl. One day he was there at the table, chain smoking and pursuing his favourite hobbies: bitching about the world he saw printed in the newspaper, and staring out the window. Next day something snapped, I guess, because me and Momma woke up to find him gone, with nothing but his smokes, his shoes and the car. Left an envelope with a hundred bucks on the night table beside my bed.

"She searched for him for awhile. She called around to all his friends; they hadn't heard from him. Or they lied. She tried to file a missing person's report, but the police said it didn't count when someone left on their own accord. She even put an ad in the paper. We got an unsigned postcard from New Mexico about six months later. Could have been from him. Hardly mattered at that point, because by then, Mom had shacked up with a new guy who'd just come into town.

"There always was something strange about the new guy, but after Daddy's silences, I guess she found some comfort in Rick. Maybe his decisiveness, or something."

Her gaze wandered over the table to my wallet, where she began tugging absent-mindedly at a stray thread. Then she drew her hand back quickly and apologized with a limp smile.

"Anyway, he seemed the protective type. Strong. Quiet. Commanding. Quite a switch from Daddy, who was always going unnoticed." She stopped and met my eyes. "We thought he had 'charisma.' Ha!

"Nobody was exactly sure where he'd come from. We gave up trying to figure out after awhile. Anyway, he seemed to be sticking around, and that was good enough at the time. Mom was lonely, I was bored, and he needed some feminine company.

"I had a crush on him immediately, which suited him fine. He was dark and watchful and serious, which made him seem smarter than my dad. I figured I would help things along by calling him Daddy. It seemed to fit. He was the man with my mom, after all. He'd sit me on his lap and smooth my hair, kiss my neck. After living all that time with a ghost of a man, I loved the attention. I didn't know any better.

"He and my mom worked different schedules. She had her day shifts at the kitchen in the hospital, and he worked nights as a janitor in the bank. I was old enough to stay on my own after school, but he always seemed to want to be there with me. He spent a lot of time exercising in the daytime, running, working out on his punching bag. And when I came home, he'd ask me for back rubs. I was happy enough to help out, you know. It made me feel important, grown up.

"One time he rolled over to face me. I was scared. He held both of my hands in his big fist, and with his other hand he started rubbing my leg.

"I heard the floor creak outside the door and was about to turn toward it when Momma came through the door with a gun. Everything was really quiet for a second, and then my ears started ringing. I can't remember hearing any of what went on after that. But she must've told him to go because he did.

"Then Momma came over to the bed, held me on her lap, rocking and rocking. I thought her heart would come right out of her chest, thumping against the side of my head like that. She asked me if he'd done anything else, and I told her no, not really understanding why she was so angry. After sitting with me a few minutes, she pulled a hanky out of her jeans pocket and wrapped up the gun and walked out of the room and talked to someone on the phone. The cops, I guess."

I looked at her, tongue-tied, like she was a script in a foreign language. Why was she telling me this? I wanted to stop her, but in my second of opportunity I'd forgotten her name.

"Anyway, Rick took off. Left his things behind, not that he had much to leave. No one said much about him after that. Funny. It all just fades away, eh?"

*Helen.* I needed another drink, and I wasn't even finished my first one. I waited a few minutes, hoping she'd break into laughter and retract the whole tale.

Helen met my eyes and smirked. "Oh, God. How did I get into this? Just so you know, I don't bare my soul to every lonely truck driver I meet at western double-bills."

"There's a big contingent of us, is there?"

"You'd be surprised."

"What makes you say I'm lonely?"

"Aren't you?"

I changed the subject. This night was growing stranger by the minute. "Is your mom still alive?"

"Nope. Lung cancer. Smoked like a chimney. Been alone ever since. Attachments just aren't worth the bother. Usually," she added and winked.

A large woman in tight white pants tried to squeeze past our table and knocked over the remains of my beer. She screeched and tried to block it from running off the table with two ragged coasters, which proved to be as efficient as folding an octopus into a shoe box. Helen offered a lopsided smile. I left and returned with a length of paper towel for Helen and a dish rag for the table. Then I shooed the intruder away with as much tact as I could muster, wiped my seat and sat down.

"Sorry about that," I said.

"Never apologize, never explain. Especially when it wasn't your fault." Helen winked again. "Well, now. I've come to the end of my story and your beer is gone. This is your opportunity to split without making me feel like I've bored you to death. I'm going to have one of those dreams tonight where you find you've walked into a crowd of people and you forgot to put your pants on. The I've-Said-Too-Much dream." She stretched her lips across her teeth, squared her elbows on the table, folded her hands and lengthened her neck, fairly dragging my eyes into the cavern behind the snaps of her shirt. "How long has it been for you?"

"Huh?" I asked, afraid I knew what she meant.

"Has there been anyone since your wife?" Then, adjusting her line of attack, "Have you been laid since the seventies?"

I flushed, suddenly virginal.

"I didn't think so." She slid her hands to the edges of the table and gripped. She arched her back ever so slightly. I excused myself to the bathroom, and when I opened the door again, Helen was nodding something at the woman in white pants. She caught my eye, strode toward me, and together we made for the street.

IT WAS LIBERATING, IN THAT WAY ADMITTING A DIRTY SECRET absolves you of its burden.

We pulled the truck over near a dumpster, and left the engine on for heat and something to muffle the silence. Had we been in a more regular place with curtains drawn and a locked door, I might have been ambushed by fear and humiliation. But we were not.

Everything was delicious until the rock came through the window.

Before I knew which way was up, a big man, square as a cinder block, reached through the passenger window, unlocked the door, and hauled Helen out by the shoulder.

"Carmen! Get out of there, you worthless whore!"

I froze. For a second I wondered if I'd had a stroke, or if someone had slipped something in my drink.

"Babysitting, eh? Is that what this is called?" He started dragging her backward as she stumbled to get her footing. "When are you going to realize?" He left the sentence hanging, too angry or too inarticulate to finish it.

"Hey!" I pulled up my shorts, slipped into my boots and jumped out, with an armful of her clothes.

He seemed to have forgotten about me. He dropped Helen, who finally found her feet and hunkered down near the dumpster like a child afraid of the dark. The cinder block roared back and grabbed me by the hair before I could take another breath. Helen scooted along behind, grabbed what clothes she could and disappeared back into the truck.

The punch didn't hurt, so much as shatter every sense in my head. "I can't count the number of times I've had to do this. I almost feel sorry for you assholes." The second one came like a nuclear blast.

"Don't believe a word she told you," he called out into the night, as he tucked in his shirt over his ample stomach and ambled away. "And don't bother coming home this time, either!" he shouted to her, the words trailing off as he walked on and my hearing submerged in a chorus of bells.

Helen — or whatever her name was — was gone when I found my way back to the truck. As was my wallet.

*Gregorio, do you fear the dust in your throat?*

·

PART II

MARY & DARREN

·

## ❧ *Nine*

OVER THE FOLLOWING WEEK, RANDY CAME TO ACCEPT THE idea of Mary moving out, much as one comes to accept the idea of a malignant tumour. Life would be different and strange from now on, irreversibly changed.

One day when Darren had gone out for awhile, Randy managed to steal Mary away for a talk. He took her to the river where they had paddled every summer when Mary was young. Travelling south past the underground coal fires of Cumberland and the cool dark banks of Content Bridge, he and Mary would sing: *Who do the hoodoos under the August moon? We do the voodoo that carves the rock to dune.* They'd sleep on the high ground, the wind *sh-sh*-ing through their tent, and wake in the morning to rub the wood smoke from their eyes: sand in their shoes, sand in their hair, sand in their morning tea.

This time, they took the long way out, past the empty farm houses and sagging barns, the scrubby squares of caraganas where a district school once stood. They geared down for the long descent over the sandy road wending through sage and pine and a latticework of dry, cracked earth.

At their favourite spot, the river was wide and lazy, and the air smelled of fish. Willows crowded the edge like anxious spectators, and the sandy banks were collapsing slowly, as though an outer skin had been peeled away. Autumn was blushing in the leaves, and the wind ticked with an insect metronome. They slammed their doors, the claps rattling through the lonely hills.

"I don't want to meddle in your life, Mary—" Randy began.

"But I'll bet you're going to." Mary smiled. She began trudging over the heavy, wet sand, the balls of her feet violating the smooth, sparkling skin.

"I just want to be sure you're doing the right thing."

"Tough thing to know, Dad." She picked up a rock, turned it over in her hand. A perfect oval of granite, rubbed smooth as an egg down the miles of tributaries. She slipped it into her pocket and held it in the basket of her fingers like resolve. Her eyes found a particular bank of swallow nests, lingered a moment and wandered away again.

"I want to know that what you're doing is right for you. Are you ready to leave one man's house behind and move right into another's? Are you prepared for this to be the rest of your life? Because it could be, you know. Are you committed enough
to yourself to withstand a commitment to someone else?"

Without looking at her father, Mary took off her shoes and dug ten pink toes into the sand.

"Is he good to you?"

"Could anyone be good enough for me in your book, Dad?" She flopped down on her back, and stared at the empty sky. After a few moments, Randy joined her.

One July afternoon a long time ago, Mary had thrown on her favourite pair of yellow plastic flip-flops, each with a flower between her toes, and she and Randy had gone down to the river and walked up around the big bend to a place in the shade where the river grass grew long and there were good rocks for hiding.

They spent the better part of an hour, the chalky smell of sand in their noses and the grit working its way under their toenails and in behind their teeth while they peered over a gentle bank and into the smallest pools. Fry by the dozens nosed their way into the sediment, flirted with the alien surface and chased each other nose to fin around their tiny liquid universe. Mary had marvelled at the continuity of water, how, agitated, it would roll in the riffles and tumble out into the pools, gentle and — though she didn't have the words for it — calm, like it hoped no one was looking. Then out it would go again into the riffles. How, to the fish, it was all calm and cool and providing, and they didn't know there was such a thing as a boundary because they'd never been outside one, how there was nothing to do all day but eat bugs and listen to that hum down in their bellies or somewhere that told them to chase this fish away and take this other for its own. She had admired their patience, how their every moment was full to bursting with the single necessary task of being fish.

Then: *kyew, kyew, kyew.* A large white bird hovering a hundred yards upstream with a glare fierce as winter, shuddering in invisible winds. Long, slender wings braced in lift, black claws poised.

Randy had held his breath in wonder. He'd seen his share of ospreys along the Fraser and points westward, but here on the Red Deer?

Then, like a kite jerked mercilessly earthward, the bird fell to the river's surface and climbed skyward again with a silver fish that convulsed once, then froze, stunned by the air. A drop of blood fell to the water.

A rare thing. A marvellous thing. Randy had given thanks to no one in particular. Then he remembered his little girl. He looked down to find her eyes wide open and staring.

"Oh, Mary. That fish, he —"

She had gaped at him. And he hadn't known what to say.

The red blood vanished in the water, eddied by seaward momentum. Mary fell asleep that night in her father's lap on the couch, dreaming she could breathe water.

But that was a very long time ago. For now, both Randy and Mary knew there was nothing more to say. After an hour or so of companionable silence, they packed up, headed back to town and straight for a gas station, where Randy bought two take-out coffees for their drive around the half-dozen apartment buildings in town.

THEY FOUND A TWO-BEDROOM UNIT IN THE CENTRE OF TOWN on a main road. Not that Juniper Butte had many other roads, and Mary's rusty unreliable hatchback being what it was, central seemed prudent. And two bedrooms because it would be good for her to know there was a door to close behind her if she needed it. Heat and light included for five hundred per. Randy gave her the first month's rent, and for the damage deposit she used the money she'd been saving to buy a new light table. Before the afternoon was out, the deal was done.

They were loading the extra couch from the basement into the trailer when Darren came home from Calgary.

"Green velvet. Randy, I hadn't realized you were such a swinger." He came around behind Mary, put his hand on her stomach and kissed the back of her neck. She looked at her father shyly.

"Darren, instead of mauling my daughter, how about making yourself useful?"

Darren set down his shrink-wrapped boxes of computer paraphernalia on the lawn. "What's up?"

"Dad helped find us a place this afternoon. We've got a two-bedroom in Riverbend Estates, over on Third. We can move in tonight."

Darren looked first at Mary, then at Randy.

"Now that's service, eh?" Randy grinned. "I've paid your first month's rent, and that's fine. But you'd be well-advised to pay Mary back some of her art supply fund that she used for the deposit. I know where you live."

Darren said nothing and took up an end of the couch.

THEY STOOD AMONG THE BOXES AND BAGS NOT KNOWING where to begin. It was already ten by the time the last armload had come through the front door and Randy left them on their own, the click of the door like the last sentence of a book.

Or the first. It had all happened so quickly that nothing had been packed very well. And besides, Mary thought, they were only going up the street. That had meant plenty of lazy man's loads with clothes draping off shoulders and kitchen utensils in pockets. Ripped boxes and grocery bags. All of it had been pitched into three general heaps: living room, kitchen and bedrooms.

Now neither Mary nor Darren felt much like dealing with it. Mary thought Darren was a bit too sullen for the demands of the occasion. She chalked it up to how quickly things had unfolded, and perhaps, too, how little input he'd been given. But she and Randy had meant it to be a pleasant surprise. She thought Darren should be grateful.

"This is too much. I'm going to get a beer. I'll be back in a bit, okay?"

It took Mary a moment to absorb what Darren had said. "You're leaving?"

"Yeah. I'll be back soon. I just need a break from this for a bit." He patted his pocket for his car keys. "Oh, right, I guess I'll need the key for this place. Do you have my copy?"

She stared at him, a study in bemusement and horror.

He took her shoulders in his hands. "Baby. I just need a change of scenery. I'm sure you want to dive right into this stuff. I don't. I'll just get in your way. Okay?" He tipped up her chin to kiss her on the lips. She didn't respond. "Come on. What's the matter?"

"What's the matter?" She was genuinely surprised. "I have just moved in with a man — you and I have moved in together — and I am being left to 'tidy up'? What, am I your housing service and your maid, too?"

"I'm not abandoning you. I just want a little pick me up before we start."

She pulled away and shook her head. "Not exactly a great

start to things." She threw up her hands. "But whatever. Do what you like." She turned from him, shoved a milk crate of books out of the way and repositioned the couch in the centre of one living room wall.

Darren watched her from behind, eyeing the muscles in her thighs tensing and stretching with the efforts of her display. He lunged, grabbed her around the waist and laughed. "Okay. Enough with the Hercules act. I won't go. Happy?" He kissed her squarely on the mouth before she could answer.

She extracted her lips. "Don't stay on my account."

"*Don't stay on my account,*" he mocked, smiling. "Just don't expect your life to be worth living if you go, right?"

"No, Darren, it's not like that. It's about —"

"I know, I know. I get the picture. Equal efforts, all that. I'll stay. Okay? I'll stay." He opened his mouth to drop in his car keys and looked at her from the corner of his eye. She didn't appreciate the joke. Instead, he opened the patio door and put the keys on the balcony. "Okay? I'm staying."

"Right. Because God knows how you could ever find those keys again." She folded her arms in blockade against him.

"It's a gesture. Cut me some slack." He forcibly unfolded her arms and put them around his own waist. "Better?"

A smile slowly crept across her face.

His hands went to her top button. "I'll stay here. And

we'll bless our new surroundings instead." She made no move to stop him.

Later, in the late-summer-night heat, the two lay under a single sheet on a mattress in the centre of the floor. Darren's breaths were already regular and long. Mary traced her finger along the long line from the hollow in his throat to his navel, painting him. She gathered the warmth of his belly in the palm on her hand, then placed her hand on herself and joined him in sleep.

RANDY PAID A VISIT THE NEXT SATURDAY MORNING WITH fresh blueberry muffins from Dutchy's, a third-generation bakery around the corner whose annual run on hot-cross buns was rumoured to keep the store going for the whole year. He clanked up the metal stairs, past the stains on the carpet and smudged wallpaper, to number 307. He rang the doorbell and put his finger over the peephole.

Quick barefoot steps; a pause. Then, "Who is it?"

"Good girl. Just testing you."

Open flew the door, and before he could say hello, Mary's arms were wrapped tightly around her father's neck. He kissed her on the cheek, peeled her off him, and passed her the paper bag of muffins. "Careful, they're hot."

"You're so sweet. You must have been up with the birds." She winked at him, stretched to set the bag on the table, and pulled him in by the hand.

Randy looked around. Cinder block bookshelves, an ancient black and white TV propped up on a milk crate, Mary's portrait of Hank Williams near the patio doors, and above the couch, in mismatched frames, two Ansel Adams photos torn from a calendar. An old phone table painted fire engine red stood in the corner adorned with a newly blooming cactus. A box of paints cowered nearby. He picked up Mary's sketch book from the kitchen table, brushed off a thin layer of dust and opened to the last entry: an outline of a train emerging from a garage door. It was dated September 5th. He raised his eyebrows appraisingly, and she grabbed the book from his hands, tsk-tsking as she did so.

"I didn't say I thought it had been awhile since you drew anything. I didn't say that." He smiled ironically. "The place looks great. Where'd you get the cactus?"

Mary padded over to the corner and picked up the heavy clay pot. "Darren dug this up when he went back to Lethbridge to duke it out one more time with his boss. I think it was just an excuse to traipse through the badlands, myself. He loves it out there."

Randy nodded appreciatively. The badlands only accept a man who's good company to himself.

Mary brushed her fingers over the palm of the cactus and pressed her thumb in the moist soil. "Ten bucks say I kill it. I can never quite bring myself to believe that cactuses actually don't want water. I think of them as being too shy to ask or something, so I sneak them some on the sly. I'll love this thing to death."

She put the pot back on the stand and ducked into the kitchen to boil the kettle and arrange the muffins on a plate. They stepped out onto the patio and sat down at a plastic table to eat.

A calm Saturday morning, full of sunshine and promise, and quiet before the bleating of traffic. A small boy kicked at a soccer ball by himself in the courtyard, stopping alternately to pull up his socks, tie up his laces or pick at the remains of an earthworm-caked sidewalk. A girl about his age zoomed by on a skateboard, scooped up his ball in mid-roll, and the two took off down the alley and into traffic. Mary picked at the edges of her muffin, then set it aside. She leaned back in the chair, cupped her tea in two hands on her belly and dropped her head back on the top of the chair. Her hair reached nearly to the seat, her pale skin — a gift from her mother — warming in the low sun of morning. She swallowed, and her throat moved like a shoulder shrugging under a sheet.

"There was a scientist once who believed you could tell if a man was lying by the way a vein pulsed in his lower leg," Randy offered.

She picked up her heavy head. "Do tell. What on earth reminded you of that?"

"I can see one of the veins in your neck."

"And? What does it tell you?"

"Don't know if the theory applied to necks. Or women."

They laughed, and Randy topped up her tea. They sat in silence, the sun warming their lizard souls.

"Where's Darren?" Randy asked finally.

"Gone to High River to visit Chris, his photographer friend. He's got a project in the hopper he wants them to work on."

Randy regarded his daughter. "You look really good. Happy."

"You say that like you're surprised." She continued smiling until she realized he was indeed surprised. Then her face pinched. "What?"

"Nothing."

"Don't 'nothing' me. 'Fess up."

Randy looked away to the courtyard where an old woman was stepping carefully through the grass clutching a plastic shopping bag to her chest.

"Earth to Dad!" She smiled uncertainly. Her throat tightened.

Randy looked back. "You think this is going to work out?"

"There's no reason it won't. I wouldn't be here if I thought it wasn't."

"Spoken like a woman cornered."

Mary's sufferance snapped. "Well, what am I supposed to say, Dad? Listen, I know you're having trouble with the empty nest thing, but it's time for me to get out in the world, okay?"

Randy dropped his eyes. He followed the ridges and grooves in the pattern of the table, and studied the dust collected in miniature drifts. It was everywhere, coating all the shine.

"Mary, it's just that I know what it's like to love someone so much you forget where the line is between you. So much that it becomes less like love and more like self-preservation. Survival. Only, with a lot of people, it gets short-circuited somewhere along the way and becomes ownership. And with ownership comes certain expectations."

He paused, fiddled with greasy muffin paper splayed on his plate. He dropped his voice then looked directly at her.

"Your mother was badly abused before she came to Juniper Butte. She still had the welts when I met her. And the thing is, the guy she was with was a bastard, but he wasn't a psychopath. In fact, he was pretty charming. He believed he owned her, Mary, and what do you do when something you own misbehaves? You curse on it, you kick it, you jerk its chain."

Mary's eyes narrowed and her face dimmed. "You never told me that. Why didn't you tell me?"

"I don't know, Mary."

"Yes, you do. You seem to have a reason for everything. Drives me nuts." Her voice was hardening.

"A lot of things go unsaid about a life, Mary. I didn't want you remembering her like that."

"Like how?"

"Less than what she should have been. Unwhole."

"Unwhole? It mustn't have been her fault."

"No, that's not what I meant. Truth be told, I thought I could fix it all just by unremembering it."

"Except you never did."

"No."

She dropped her hand to the frayed edge of her shorts and pulled at a loose thread. "Why are you bringing it up now?"

Randy pulled his chair out from behind the table and lay his hands on her knees. "Mary, I know you don't want to hear this. God knows, I don't want to be the one to be telling you. Maybe I don't need to. But I've seen it happen, honey, so at the risk of sounding foolish — or hell, maybe even pushing you away — I'm going to say this. The first time he shoves you, or calls you a name, you burn with indignation. Then after that, when you realize you've survived and you become proud of your toughness, then you're really in trouble. You get high on martyrdom, see? You, Mary Thompson, have your mother's survival instinct, but I will not see you broken the way she was." He paused, considering whether to stray into such heavily guarded territory. "What about that last sketch in your book, there?"

"What do you mean?"

"I mean, your art seems to have taken a back seat since our friend moved into town. Don't you think you might regret that?"

A surge of something like anger and something like guilt ran through Mary, and she coiled like a snake. "That's none of your business. You should know better than to bring that up."

Randy relented. "Just be careful, okay?" He looked at her levelly. "And I'd like a key to the place."

Mary took two measured breaths. "It's not a bad idea, but given the tone of this conversation, I'm not sure how I feel about it."

"Blame it on your old man's paranoia if you like. It would just give me some piece of mind."

Mary watched him for a time, then slowly went to a kitchen drawer and returned with a single key on a rubber Harley Davidson key chain. She dangled it in his face, then dropped it into his open hand.

"Thanks."

They sat a time in the swelling sun, regarding each other.

# ❧ Ten

MARY SAT ON A STOOL BEHIND THE TILL, HER ELBOWS planted on her knees and her chin in her hands. A slow Monday morning. Up the road at the hardware store, pickups idled in the lot, parked head to foot as men inside, desperate for purpose but waiting for inspiration and the morning's caffeine to kick in, volleyed plans and jokes back and forth through the open windows. A fat man in a heroic belt trotted across the road from the take-out window with a bulging paper bag. A brittle old lady with powdered skin and cobweb hair caned her way to the post office, and the town clerk unlocked the door to the library. The heat through the plate glass window was lulling Mary to sleep, and as she watched two magpies chase each other from light pole to tree branch to power line, she stretched like a cat in the sun.

The door jingled open behind her and the letters IGA on the glass door flickered across her face in shadow. She pulled her white grocer's coat around her and stood up off the chair.

"Hi, Mrs. Deutcher. Quiet morning out there."

"Like a morgue after hours. How are you, little one? Can you help me with my list?"

Mary helped the woman negotiate the aisles of protective undergarments and rheumatism ointment, collected a couple of boxes of chocolates for her granddaughters in Swift Current, and a small bottle of tonic for her gin. She rang in the order and piled it in the woman's wire cart, dangling her cane off the back.

Both of them jumped as Darren roared by in his Camaro.

Mrs. Deutcher wagged her head. "That's your new fella, isn't it?"

Mary nodded.

"He was nosing around here before, wasn't he? And then what? He met you and couldn't tear himself away, is that it?"

Mary smiled. "Something like that."

"Is he good to you, girl? Because if there's one thing I've learned, it's that life is too short to be settling for halfwits and men who don't dance. You gotta make them pay attention and realize what they've got in you, because sometimes they're a little lazy. Then all of a sudden, one day they wake up, they're sixty years old and they don't have a clue who's been cooking their pot roast all these years, but they're too old and scared to do anything about it. And the only good in that is the I-told-you-so. Okay, dear?"

She patted Mary's hand and trundled out through the door without waiting for an answer, almost bodychecked by Sara who was rushing in.

"Sorry, Mrs. Deutcher." Sara dropped her purse behind the counter and swivelled back toward the door. "Here, let me help you with that." She held the door open with her elbow and pushed the cart through with the other hand. Mrs. Deutcher lunged for her cane as Sara disappeared. A few minutes passed before Mary heard the old woman's '82 Cadillac grumble off down Pincher Street. Sara came back through and took a deep, urgent breath.

"I was beginning to feel stood up. It's ten-thirty. Where were you?" Mary smiled as she eased herself back on her perch.

"I know, sorry. You've been worked to the bone here without me, I can tell." Sara squatted down and rustled through her purse. "I was getting this." She passed a small brown paper parcel to Mary, who squinted suspiciously.

"Take it," Sara said. "It's your housewarming present."

Mary took the package and opened it, carefully undoing

the string bow, and peeling the tape from the paper like an orange peel.

"My God," Sara roared. "It'll take three days to open the presents at your wedding. It's meat-wrapping paper, for Christ's sake. Rip it open."

Mary unfolded the tissue paper and held up three pairs of thong underwear: lime green, powder grey and black. The door tinkled again and Mary snapped them behind her back and nodded to two guys in electric company uniforms. They headed for the pop cooler at the back of the store. Mary shook the underwear in Sara's face and smiled.

"Jesus, Sara. I lost a year off my life just then. My housewarming present, eh? More like Darren's, I'd say."

"Got any root beer?" A voice from the back.

"Hang on," Mary yelled and rounded the corner to help them. She returned in a minute, blushing.

"They wanted to know where we keep the whips and handcuffs. I gave them directions to your house."

Sara shoved her and sat herself up on the counter. "So tell me how this cohabitation thing is going, anyway."

Mary settled back on her stool. "It's good."

"Good." Sara stared. "And?"

"And what? I know it's surprised the hell out of everyone. Not least of whom is me, just for the record. And I guess you're never really *ready*. Life just presents itself, then you see it through. Or you don't."

"Spoken like someone recently knocked up." A male voice, a couple of feet behind her head.

"Jesus!" Mary jumped off her stool. "You guys are a plague. Give me your money." She rang in their pops, then looked up at their grinning faces. "Oh, shut up. Go away." She sent them off with their change and a wink.

"That's very deep, Mary," Sara resumed. "Your maturity is duly noted. Now drop the bullshit and give me the details."

Mary tore off the receipt from the till and balled it up. "Like what?"

"Like what? You shack up, and suddenly you forget how to be a girl? Is he a slob? Does he fart in bed? What does he do with his pocket change? I want the complete profile." Sara sat farther back on the counter, and settled in for the narrative.

Mary examined the front of her work jacket, ran her fingers along the wrinkles of the hem. She had a sudden urge to bolt home to the ironing table. Or maybe just to bolt home. But she couldn't lie to Sara. There was no point. The woman was psychic litmus paper. "Well, there's one thing on my mind."

Sara squinted. "What's that?"

Mary sighed. "My dad told me some things recently about my mom before the two of them got together."

"What do you mean?"

"She, I guess, was in a nasty relationship before she

showed up to teach here. I think the guy used to beat her up pretty bad. Anyway, my dad took it all personally. I guess anyone would. And—" She drew in a breath and searched for the words.

"And?" Sara was impatient now.

"And it makes him protective about me. He doesn't want me ending up like her, I guess."

"Why would he say something like that? Has Darren done something. Mary?"

"No. No." Mary paused. "It's just —"

"Mary. Come on."

"Stop. Let me tell my story." She pushed her hair back from her head and scratched her scalp, as though massaging her brain into action. "I just brought it up with Darren one day. I tried to be cool about it. I wanted him to know a bit about where I came from. I think about my mom a lot, you know, and I don't have a whole lot to go on."

Sara chewed the inside of her cheek.

"And when I started to tell him what my dad had told me, he just —" Mary's face contorted.

"He just what?"

"I don't know, he changed the subject." Mary shrugged. "Didn't seem very interested."

Despite her friendly evasion, the conversation still rang in her ears. She and Darren had just finished supper and had pushed aside the chili bowls and crusts of bread to make more room for their elbows and beer. Mary watched Darren pick at his teeth with the corner of a matchbook.

"That was good," he said, tossing the wet cardboard into the centre of the table. "I never thought about putting black beans in chili."

"Lethbridge is not exactly the centre of the culinary world."

"And Juniper Butte is?"

Mary chuckled. "More than Lethbridge, I reckon. It's all those franchises down there. Obliterates your sense of possibility."

"Uh-huh." He took a pull of his beer.

She winked. Then her face changed. "My dad told me something about my mom the other day that's really stuck with me."

"Oh, yeah? What's that?" Darren yawned, passed a hand over his face and sniffed.

"Well, before my dad she was with this guy who used to beat her up."

"Yeah?"

"Yeah." Mary waited for him to ask for more. He didn't. She continued. "He wouldn't tell me much about it. Just that the guy was a creep — obviously —" she rolled her eyes, "and that he thought she kind of got used to it. And that it was kind of like an infection you get used to. I think that's what he said. Anyway. He'd never told me about it because he didn't want me worrying. And he wanted to protect me or something. I don't know. He didn't elaborate. Am I making any sense?"

"I suppose."

"Isn't that creepy?"

Darren furrowed his brow and shrugged. "Not really."

"What do you mean, 'not really'?"

"Well, it's pretty common, actually."

"Doesn't make it right."

"It's not about being right."

"What?"

"You said it was creepy. Shitty, yes. But creepy, no. Read the papers. Watch the tube. People piss each other off. They get mad. They lose their tempers."

"Yeah, except women throw their anger into scrubbing the floor or they vent at a friend."

"Oh, please. Women hit just as much as men."

"Ha!"

"They do. 'Domestic violence,'" Darren said the words as though he thought them ridiculous, "goes both ways, you know."

Mary shook her head. "That's like saying poor people should pay as much in taxes as rich people because they both use sidewalks."

"What? All I'm saying is that there are two sides to every story. Cause and effect."

"Yeah, but the cause is —" Mary slumped in her chair. "Never mind."

Darren picked at the label on his beer. Then Mary remembered. "This is not sounding like someone who went to jail defending his battered ex-girlfriend."

Darren's eyes met hers. He looked long and hard. Defending someone doesn't mean being blind to reality."

"But men and women don't have —" She couldn't find the words to finish her sentence. Finally, she said, "Would you ever hit me?"

"No."

"Are you sure?"

"Come on. What do you take me for?" Darren pushed back from the table, strode to the kitchen, folded his arms and strode back. "Listen. Don't fuck this up, okay? We've got a good thing here. You know I wouldn't hurt you. I've never stood for it in the past from other people. I was just saying that people hurt each other in complex ways. I obviously don't know anything about your mom or the asshole she was with, but there's probably more to the story than your dad was letting on. Probably more than she even told him. Don't go getting paranoid. And don't put words in my mouth."

"I wasn't, I —"

"Okay? I've said my piece. Now relax. I'm sorry about your mother. It must have been hard for her."

Mary's breaths were small. She couldn't look at him. He stepped toward her and rested a hand on her head. "Listen. I haven't told you this yet, but I love you, all right?"

Mary looked up. "Strange time to tell me."

He gripped her shoulders in two hands, coaxed her up from the chair and held her. "What's past is past, okay?"

The exchange had left Mary feeling as though Darren's life was a locked room, off limits. It made her lonely. She told Sara none of this, though.

Sara shook her head. "My, my. What have you got going on there?"

"Well, you asked. But that's just a little shitty part of it," Mary said, now smiling again enthusiastically. "The rest is great."

Sara crooked a skeptical eyebrow.

"Okay. It was strange deciding who got which side of the bed. I was sort of into not *having* sides. You know, *our* room, *our* bed — everything shared. But he insists on having the control panel — the alarm clock, the lamp — and the bed is right up against the wall, so I feel a bit like I'm being supervised. I think I'll lobby for a bedside table of my own, just like you see on the cough syrup commercials." With the guilt of a pilfering employee, she peered over the windowsill for any impending interruptions.

"And he puts the soap on the tub next to the tap, and I hate that because I have to bend through the shower spray and it rinses the conditioner out of my hair."

"And?"

"And he leaves cups and spoons right-side up in the dish rack, which drives me nuts because the goop dries in them, so I'm forever going through, checking his work after he's done. I've become an inspector, Sara, and that bothers me. Sort of."

"And?"

"And? God! I don't know. He's a guy. I'm getting used to him. And I think I'm having fun. End of story." She tossed her little ball of paper in the garbage.

"No it's not. How's the sex?"

Mary shook her head slowly, incredulously. "What is this? The Inquisition? Oh, the indignity."

"Indignity my ass, girlfriend. I am entitled to know absolutely everything about your boyfriend. It serves two purposes. One, it lets me live vicariously through you. And two, it lets me know when to hire the assassin. Get it?"

"Between you and my father, I'm lucky to ever get laid. Assassin? What kind of talk is that?"

"Realistic, my dear. No matter how wonderful this guy is right now, more than likely, you two will split up. If he's lucky, it will be amicable. If it's not, we'll have to kill him. But the thing is, and I've seen this happen," Sara's hand twisted in the air to the sound of her own warning, "girls get into these demanding relationships, stop spending time with their real friends — that is, the ones who don't want to sleep with them — and then, when there's no more relationship, they're left naked in a snowstorm, and feeling sad and guilty for putting themselves there. So they rekindle their female friendships, vowing never to be so stupid again. This helps them get back their life and vitality, refreshing their interest in, and attractiveness to, men, and the whole thing starts again. It's ugly. I don't want to see that happen to you. Now cough up."

Mary grimaced. "I don't know, Sara. I'd rather not."

Sara sat back, mildly hurt. "What's going on? Suddenly you're too good for gossip?"

"No. Just — not here. You know. Another time."

Sara nodded slowly. "Whatever."

"No, really. I promise. It's just — Darren and I are still getting used to each other, okay?"

"But you're happy?"

"I'm happy."

"Any signs of work on his horizon?"

"Not yet. It all takes time."

"And you? You still painting?"

"Yeah. I still feel kind of weird doing it when he's around, so I try to sneak in time when he's out. But yeah, I'm mucking around."

Sara studied her for a time. "Okay," she said, and retired to the back to stock shelves.

DARREN STRETCHED OUT ON THE HOOD OF HIS SILVER Camaro, undid the top few buttons of his shirt and took a deep drag on his cigarette. Sun spilled through dying poplar leaves like river water through an old man's fingers, and a single blackbird *konk-a-ree-d* in the thick afternoon distance. Smoke tickled his lungs and his whole body warmed to the suggestion of summer.

His father would shit his pants, he thought, if he saw Darren now. The sloth, he'd say. Living off a young girl's father, what a disgrace. As if he were one to talk, the pig. A smart enough man, but utterly lacking in ambition, and too lazy to pick up the TV dinner trays, or even wash himself very often. No wonder Darren's mother left them both for the city. She probably thought any son of his father's was destined to be a halfwit at best. Probably resented the years she'd given them, holding them close to her breast like a karmic IOU, a dowry for a life immeasurably more glamorous, lovely and bejewelled waiting breathlessly in the wings. And who could blame her? Her two boys — one husband and one son — were a woman's shame, and she let them know as much, first through sputtering attempts at discipline, then wordless accusations, then finally, her absence. She removed her forgiveness and her hope.

Darren laced his fingers behind his head and traced clouds across the sky: a dragon, a rowboat, a horseshoe melting westward.

His mother had taken an apartment in the east end of Calgary and finally grew heavier and heavier until she slipped in the bathtub one day and died. The weight of her fall had knocked plaster from the downstairs neighbour's ceiling. His father just kept eating and farting and watching Wheel of Fortune until the tick-tick-ticking of the wheel drove Darren out of the house and into the waiting arms of Sandra.

*Sandra, Sandra, burning bright, out of mind and out of sight.* Sandra was the queen of backyard barbecues and horseshoe tournaments, long summer nights on the porch with iced tea and bug dope. There were generations of mechanics and crossing guards and gas jockeys twinkling in Sandra's deep brown eyes, latent in her loins, and the beauty of her was that she didn't know the half of it. She'd taken to casseroles and cookies as though she'd been ordained for it by God, and nothing gave her greater joy than a smile smeared across the face of an appreciative man. Her daughters would all be cheerleaders and they'd all come home on Sundays with their toddlers and their yellow dogs. Sandra was nothing like Darren's mother. Didn't question him, didn't pester him. Hardly asked anything of him at all, except the chance to make him happy.

Until the baby came along. Darren and Sandra were two years gone from high school and still waiting for the topography of the future to unfold. Darren was growing glossy and fat under Sandra's care, and Sandra had begun to feel comfortable, as though the world were melting a perfect spot right around the two of them.

Three weeks after she'd missed her first period, she mustered up enough nerve to drive to the pharmacy in the next town. That afternoon, sitting in her mother's bathroom with two bare feet up on the bathtub, a breeze blowing in from the river through the window and a white wand with two blue lines between her fingers, she looked into the future and it looked very much like today: every night opening like a long, velvet glove, quiet moments on the porch, the cheerleaders, the yellow dogs. She cleaned up and called Darren at work.

She hadn't understood. Not the pulls toward Darren's lap when he and his buddies were drinking beer, not the smiles and lazy hugs after supper. No, she hadn't understood anything. Darren was not about to suffer the guilt of another woman and her damned lost ambitions, as though it had anything to do with him. When she whimpered, he told her she was pathetic. And when she cried, he backhanded her a few times across her forever-open mouth, threw some shirts into a box, and left.

He'd been prepared to forget things and just move on until her old man showed up. Trust a meddling father to fuck up everything. She'd brainwashed him with all sorts of bullshit about how she'd been pushed around and yelled at, how her life had been endangered, how the injuries had made her lose her baby. The judge — a woman, of course — swallowed the whole thing. Darren got an all-expenses paid visit to Drumheller. One year: aggravated assault.

He was sorry things had worked out the way they did, but what else could he have done? He certainly wasn't going to be tied down by some screaming, bawling youngster and a wife growing fatter by the hour.

Things would never get that far with Mary, and what she didn't know wouldn't hurt her.

Darren left the sky to its own devices and got back in the car.

## ❧ *Eleven*

MARY AND DARREN LAY PROPPED UP AGAINST THE WALL WITH four ratty pillows between them. Against their bellies they held glasses of wine in mismatched pewter goblets. Candlelight flickered from every possible surface: short, red-smelling candles on the dresser fluttering in the ghost breeze through the window; skinny, anemic candles melting onto bare board shelves staggered up the wall.

Mary affected a dreadful Australian accent. "Tonight on Lifestyles of the Rich and Famous, we visit the Boyce-Thompson household in a highly sought-after end-of-hall, two-bedroom suite in Riverbend Estates in picturesque Juniper Butte. Funny the 'Riverbend' part, as there's no river for miles, but you know the rich and their eccentricities. Meet Darren and Mary as they recline with —"

Darren balanced his wine glass on a shelf just within reach, and slid a hand across Mary's mouth.

"—a hand hicked early hintage of hine habernet —"

He pulled his hand away and quickly covered her mouth with his until she stopped talking and smiled underneath his kiss. Then she pulled back. "You don't like my accent? I thought I was brilliant."

Darren kissed her again, this time easing the wine glass out of her hand and sliding over on top of her. He pushed his nose up and under her bangs and kissed her face slowly, deliberately, moving lower, and stopping to taste the wine on her breath. Tiny breaths, coming quick and short. He moved lower still, working his tongue from the corner of her mouth underneath her jaw, down to the hollow beneath her throat and between her breasts. He pulled the sheet over himself like a bandit, and her lower stomach tensed as his knees worked hers farther apart. Still working his tongue, he traced a circle around her navel, rasping his unshaven chin over the pale field of her belly while her toes curled and uncurled.

They made love again, surprised at themselves. Then they propped themselves up with their wine and giggled.

Mary paused as she let her breathing fall into sync with Darren's. Cold little blue breaths in; long, slow pink breaths out. She looked down at her small, sloping breasts, her nipples puckered in the breeze, and was surprised by her lack of shame. Darren caught her looking, and curled his finger in a lock of her hair and draped it over her right shoulder, just so. He took a mouthful of wine and turned his head toward the wall.

The chain around his neck glinted in the candlelight, and she leaned across him to take a closer look.

The chain held a ring of the thinnest gold, with a tiny diamond perched atop a thick setting of silver carved on either side like tulips. His grandmother's wedding ring.

Mary looked closely at the diamond, tracing it with her finger. Then she stopped and peered. "Oh, my God!" she laughed. "That gunk there. That's a piece of bread dough, isn't it?"

Darren pulled it away to inspect it himself. Mary squared herself and rested her chin on his solar plexus. "Looks like it," he said, dropping it in the plane between his chest muscles.

"Tell me about her," Mary said, her lazy head bouncing on every syllable.

"Tell me a story, Daddy?" Darren whined, mocking her. She dug in her chin until he buckled. "Ow! Okay, okay. Jesus, you're vicious." He pried his fingers under her chin and rubbed his chest.

"Well, her name was Norma Boyce. Born Norma Kowalski, November sixteen, nineteen-ought-four. Died

November fifteen, nineteen-sixty-nine. Predeceased by husband Harold. Survived by three sons and four grandsons."
He swirled his wine, held it to the candle and tried to balance it on Mary's head.

She waved it away. "That's it? And you call yourself a reporter? Where did you work, in the classified ads department?"

"Give me a break. Given the state of me, you're lucky I'm even awake." She began burrowing with her chin again and he pushed her head back with the heel of his hand.

"Okay. Let's see. I was only a week old when she died, the day before her sixty-fifth birthday. It was the great irony of her life, to have struggled through a lifetime of poverty, and then to up and die on the eve of getting her pension. Dad thought it was just her being spiteful. Myself, I think she was holding on long enough to see her beautiful baby grandson christened, and once she saw that the world was in good hands, she let go." Darren smiled at his own wit. "She died of a heart attack, poor thing."

Mary smiled. "Why do you wear this, then, if you didn't know her at all?" She twirled the ring on its chain.

He considered the question. "For years and years, I'd walked past this old trunk in the attic. I knew it belonged to Grandma, but wasn't really interested in what was in it. It was old and musty and under a pile of boxes, and it seemed like too much effort to haul it out."

"Fun kid."

"Yeah, I had better things to do."

"Like?"

"Watch TV." He smirked and took a drink of his wine. "Finally one day, I went to the effort. I cleared the stuff aside and opened the box, and once I'd recovered from the fog of mildew and Avon scented body powder, I started going through it.

"She was a devout journal-keeper, that woman. Which was amazing, because she didn't go to school past grade six, and I can't imagine her life allowing her much time for that kind of thing. Or encouragement. Anyhow, between the three boys and the farm she managed to squirrel away a few minutes for herself every day. So I learned about her from her journals."

"You read her *diary*?" Mary was horrified.

"She was dead! What I read was a historical document compiled by a member of my family."

Mary rolled her eyes.

"Anyway, if the Thought Police will let me continue," Darren flicked her in the forehead. "In fifty words or less, Norma Boyce was a good little Ukrainian girl from some ruined valley to the south. Her father didn't want her marrying into that heartbreak — crops started failing out there way before the thirties — so one day, he made her wear her best dress, bundled her up in the cart, and headed for

Lethbridge. He took her to the church and left her there with ten dollars in cash tucked into a leather pouch, an IOU for twenty head of Angus steers, and specific instructions that the first man who could prove himself trustworthy and hard-working to the pastor, could have her."

Mary couldn't believe what she was hearing. "He left her there? Like a stray cat?"

"Oh, come on. She was better off that way. Had she stayed with her father's people, the dust would have choked every child she birthed. Things were different back then."

"I don't care. She wasn't just another piece of livestock her father could trade around at will. Didn't anyone ask her what she wanted?"

"Who knows. She never wrote anything about it. This whole idea of choice is a rather new phenomenon, I think."

"Yeah, right up there with the abolition of the chastity belt." Horrified, Mary pulled a sheet up around her chin.

"Anyway, my grandfather Harold was the man for the job. He took the money and the cattle and his new bride and built up a farm on some bottomless loam out to the northeast. Norma gave him three sons. The last one — my father — was hardly dry when Harold drowned. He went out onto the river for a lost calf and went through the ice."

Mary's throat constricted, but she let him continue.

"Grandma raised her boys on her own after that, and took on a man to help out on the farm. And she may have been better off that way. Some of her earlier entries from the time Harold was still alive make mention of bruises and pulled muscles and cuts. But she wrote about it self-consciously, almost like a child in confession. I don't know, times were different then. Things would have been hard on Harold, and I guess it would have been normal for him to take it out on her." He pressed his finger to Mary's lips to keep her from speaking. "She never made much money on her own, but she kept things afloat. A few years before she died, she moved to town so she could wear her Sunday hats and drink tea with the ladies. Uncle Rich took over the farm then. I've got half a mind to do something with her journal one day. Write a book, maybe. Get Chris to throw in some landscape shots."

Mary slipped the ring, with the chain still through it, over the appropriate finger. The heavy side wheeled around toward her palm, making her fingers look bony and wasted.

"She was a big girl," Darren added. "Or at least her hands were big. She used to threaten to break you in two if you misbehaved, and there was no denying it was possible. Dad claims he saw her bend a spike into a horseshoe once, like it was a piece of licorice."

He pulled the ring from Mary's finger and got up to douse the candles. Mary watched the long, lean length of him move around the room like an alley cat, bending and blowing, bending and blowing.

It was all so overwhelming, this man, all that he knew, the space he now occupied. She wondered how there'd ever been room in her life for him. Her muscles and sinew had memorized his form, and now she waited suspended in a place closer to sleep than waking for him to come back to bed so she could curve to fit him, her knees nestled up under his backside.

He stood over her now, extinguishing the last candle on a shelf over her head. Bare naked, he leaned over her, dangling himself in her face suggestively until she turned and rolled up under the sheet.

"Oh, come on," he implored, crawling in beside her. She kept to herself and soon his breaths were coming in steady, measured volumes. She listened until the sound lulled her to sleep, too.

MARY CLAWED THE HAIR OUT OF HER EYES, PROPPED HERSELF up on one elbow and peeked out under the bedroom window blind. Sunday morning had dawned breathless, like a happy child caught spinning. She extracted Darren's threadbare white cowboy shirt from the pile of clothes at the side of the bed, slipped it on and ducked under the blind to open the window. A raven startled, and at the taffeta sound of its flapping feathers, Darren rolled to his other side. Mary slid the window down again and crept out of the bedroom, closing the door behind her.

In the kitchen, she heated a little pan of milk with a spoonful of honey, slipped on a pair of sandals and stood out on the patio, naked except for the shirt, slurping. Goose-bumps thrilled over her skin, like wingtips over the surface of water. Things were starting to turn for the season. The aspens dripped golden tears, and the long grass wrapped itself in a yellow cloak, stiffening for the winter. Even the clouds seemed reflective. She caught an old man across the yard peeking at her from behind his drapes, and with her free hand pulled the shirt tight across her thigh, then slipped back into the apartment.

"Perv," she muttered to herself, setting her cup down and sweeping her hair into a bun.

She sat on the couch, put up her feet, and basked in well-being. The thought of Darren tucked away in the bedroom — her bedroom, *their* bedroom — made her stomach tighten with longing. She was surely the first woman in history to feel so safe in her skin, so sexy and so on the verge of greatness. Just as soon as she settled into this new life, she'd start sketching again and painting. This was the place — between these four walls — where everything important would happen.

She thought of her father. All of this was because of him, and she wasn't sure she'd properly thanked him; rather, she'd spent much of their recent time together deflecting his concern. She decided to throw a little party and invite him. A housewarming party. Tonight. Why not?

Of course, there was the grocery issue. It was Sunday and with the exception of the 7-11 and the Esso, all the stores were closed. But what the hell. She could make do with canned goods and a big smile.

She padded to the kitchen and rifled through the cupboards. She and Darren hadn't been here long enough to collect the indulgent little oddities that often wind up in desperation cooking, things like canned asparagus and capers and papaya and pinto beans. She imagined these things must be as common as tomatoes in some parts of the world. But here in Alberta, where they look at you funny when you order spaghetti without meatballs, any food that came from farther away than, say, Winnipeg, was viewed with some suspicion.

The dry goods tally was: one can of chicken stew, three cans of tuna, two cans of green peas, a can of tomatoes (of course), and (she surprised herself) one can of artichoke hearts. Under the sink was a ten-pound bag of potatoes and some stray yellow onions. From the fridge, she rounded up a sweet potato, four cobs of Taber corn, and a pound of ground beef. A half block of marble cheese sulked in the corner, hardening around the edges where the plastic wrap had ripped. Sunday hash it would be. Sunday hash, fresh bread, and chocolate pie for dessert.

She brewed herself a cup of tea and opened the patio door again to let the last suggestion of summer curl up in the hidden corners of the living room. Then she started on the bread.

She tracked down the biggest bowl she could find, which turned out to be the one she'd last used as a bucket to wash the bathroom floor, down on her hands and knees with a piece of old torn bunting blanket she'd picked up at the Sally Ann. The rag now hung from a nail under the sink, stiff with old soap and dirt. They'd never know the difference. She turned on the tap and let it run over her wrist until it was warm, but not too warm, then ran some into the bowl, eyeballing how much she'd need. She tapped in a couple of spoons of brown sugar, and then a helping of yeast, and whisked the mixture with a soft whirring like a child's wind-up toy in the tub.

Mary prided herself on making bread — both for knowing how to do it in the first place, and for bothering to do so. On the other hand, she wouldn't know how to milk a cow if it walked up to her with the stool and bucket. Even cleaning a perch was a bit of a mystery. She was embarrassed about this, as if she'd been improperly schooled in the landscape that had reared her. She wanted to be able to do things for herself, and bread was one thing she could do. Besides, when you could buy it at every gas station and drugstore, there was something gratifyingly fundamentalist about baking it yourself. Something deeply good, like halter tops, cola on the front porch and cowboy hats. She smiled as colonies of yeast began blinking to the surface and warmed the kitchen with their smell. She mixed in milk, oil, an egg for luck, salt and flour, and kneaded it until the sweat trickled down her hairline and into her ears. Then she covered the bowl with a tea towel, set it to rise in the sun, glanced with guilt at her easel, then padded back to the bedroom to crawl in beside Darren, who smelled of sex and the future.

"UNFORTUNATE NAME, 'HASH'." DARREN PILED A FORK LOAD of it in his mouth, and smiled as he chewed. Mary reflected on the fact that he was the only person in the world who could chew with his mouth open and still look attractive doing so. She poured him another glass of cherry Kool-Aid, and passed along the jug.

"Anyone for some more white trash wine?" she offered. Sara and Tina topped up their glasses, but Randy passed with a flip of his hand. "I would have gotten some beer if I had thought of it," Mary apologized. "When are they going to start selling beer in the corner stores, like they do everywhere else in the free world, I wonder? I guess the thing to do is keep some on hand."

"That's a girl," Darren rubbed her between her shoulder blades and nodded to her father. "We agree on so many issues of household management."

"At times like these," Tina began, "I ask myself, 'What would Martha Stewart do?' You've decided to throw an impromptu dinner party, the good linen is out being re-woven and sterilized, global warming has made octopus caviar scarce as hens' teeth, *and* you forgot to make it to the beer store. I say, let your singing heart turn water into wine, and thank God for family and friends. And Darren, too, I guess. To the charming couple and their new home." She held up her glass in a toast, then sat down.

"Thank you, Tina. I feel like one of the family now." Darren turned and kissed Mary full on the lips.

Mary squirmed free, straightened herself, and turned to her father. Without his ball cap, his hairline lay shyly white against the ruddy line of his face. The worn cotton of his plaid shirt stretched across his chest. He looked up, stopped chewing, and sat quietly resigned to what appeared to be an impending speech.

"Dad, half the reason for doing this is because I don't think I properly thanked you for setting us up here. I know you have your doubts. Don't look away from me. I know you have your doubts about me shacking up here with this foreigner of dubious bohemian leanings, and that you think I'm entirely too young for any of it. But Darren will soon prove himself worthy of both your generosity and my affection, won't you, Darren? And when I'm a successful painter and Mister here is a world-famous author, you'll know it was all because of you." She got up from the chair and kissed her father on the cheek. "Thanks, Dad," she whispered in his ear.

"That's all right. But if it's all the same with you, I'll reserve judgement on your partner in crime until he upgrades the Kool-Aid and learns some better table manners," Randy replied, and clipped Darren between the eyes with the rest of his dinner roll.

## ❧ Twelve

THE SKY WAS A CONSTANT COMPANION FOR US THOSE YEARS on the road, and maybe that's why Mary took to painting like she did. It was a silent observer of the dramas of all of us people who roamed around down here like we owned the place. It glowed and scowled and slept and flowered, and Mary developed a sixth sense for its mood.

She'd spend hours looking out the window of the truck, staring at the sky, her chin resting on two folded hands, feet tracing circles in the air to the music on the radio. She seemed to like the flat, open spaces the best — southern Alberta with its high yellows and bleached blues, as though the sun had burned up all the colour years ago. The mountains were good, too — immediate, stern and utterly unforgiving. But the rest she seemed to suffer until we returned. The scrub hills of central British Columbia made her cranky and anxious. The deep forests west of the Fraser River sent her straight for her *Archie* comics and activity books — shrink-wrapped affairs with invisible-ink markers. Maybe it's true what they say about landscapes and the way they imprint themselves on you. The one you're born into draws you the rest of your life like a salmon returning home.

We were at a truck stop in Dead Man's Flats when I realized her strange talent for seeing landscapes. She was on summer holiday from school. I suppose she must have been about ten years old. We had stopped for a bowl of soup, still a few hours from home. The sun had just sunk behind the peaks to the west, casting the scree slopes before us in a warm pink.

The waitress brought us each a bowl of beef vegetable with a basket of biscuits still steaming from the oven. I lit into them like I'd never seen food.

I looked up to find Mary absent-mindedly fingering her spoon and gazing out the greasy window. "What's wrong, Mary?"

"Huh? Nothing." She craned her neck to see down the long stretch of highway to the east, stared for a moment, then turned her attention to her bowl. Then, a couple of spoonfuls later, she looked up and said, "They look like girls.

Standing shoulder-to-shoulder. They're wearing grey hoods. And they're blushing."

I looked at her like she'd just spoken Aramaic. "Pardon me?"

"The mountains," she said, a little testily.

"Still not following you."

She rested her spoon in her soup bowl and pushed it away. "Do you have a pen?"

I fished unsuccessfully in my shirt pocket, excused myself to the front counter, and returned to our table with a basket of crayons. I handed them to her wordlessly.

She poked around for a moment and found silver, black and pink crayons. She flipped over her paper placemat, and sketched out what looked like a chorus of gaping nuns. I looked out the window, and, to my astonishment, saw exactly what she meant. It was like slipping on a pair of glasses.

I folded the placemat and slipped it in my pocket when we left. An early edition Mary Thompson original. Complete with soup stains.

EVENTUALLY SHE ARRIVED AT THAT HIDEOUS FILTERING IN high school where she was expected to decide on her future career, and, working backwards from there, which class she might take on a particular Thursday. You couldn't take everything in a small school, and for Mary it came down to a choice between Physics and Art. She chose the latter, thinking she'd need it for when she applied to a Fine Arts program at one of the universities. Which was a shame, because the teacher — try as she might — had as much art in her as was required to refinish a bathroom. Mary got an A on everything she ever handed in, which bored her beyond reckoning. She might have done better studying equations and wondering about the boundaries of understanding.

One result of Mary being chronically underwhelmed was that she started painting with a boy in her class. Peter challenged her. Peter's talent was portraits rather than landscapes. He could capture a person's attitude and prominent features in fewer brushstrokes than it would take me to write my name. And he was never cocky about it. I suppose he knew that around these parts the only thing a boy is allowed to be cocky about is hockey, roping and his weekend conquests, not necessarily in that order. He tried his hand at hockey, but never made it past second-string defence. He seemed to prefer drawing horses to riding them. And as for the weekends? I can't say much about that. I often wondered about him and Mary. I didn't ask. But if a man has to give up his daughter, Peter was as good as any to give her up to.

The two of them spent many evenings together in my living room. Peter's own house — full of brothers, dogs and two parents who couldn't keep far enough away from each other — didn't provide much of a zone of comfort. I didn't mind. I watched when they'd let me. Or I'd wander down-town for a game of darts. Before Peter got his licence, I'd take them into Stettler once in awhile for supplies. Long shelves full of every version of paper a person could think of. Regiments of brushes. Models, easels, portfolios, adhesives, various bits of hardware. It seemed excessive to me. The two of them walked in like it was some kind of church. And I always left substantially lighter of pocket. Peter's family didn't have a lot of money. He gave me a drawing one time of a hand on a steering wheel as a kind of thank you. Mary always said hands were the hardest things to draw, and this one looked as though he'd photocopied it, it was that good. I hung it up in the garage. I don't think Mary approved of my curatorial decision, but truth was I spent a lot of time out there. It's still there, as a matter of fact.

They produced quite a body of work, Mary with her land-scapes and Peter with his faces, both of them with a special place in their palettes for red. In honour of their grade eleven graduation, the town council hung up several of their pictures in the town library. Peter's parents made a special attempt to come to the opening together and managed to leave before making a scene. The paintings were way beyond the kids' years, which silenced even the rodeo jocks.

That summer, though, things changed. Peter's dad had lost his job with the highways and was pressuring Peter to quit school and go to work to help support the family. His mother would hear nothing of it, so the parents were at each other all day. Peter took a summer job at the hardware store as a kind of compromise, and soon his painting visits dropped off to one or two a week. By the time August rolled around, he wasn't coming around at all. Mary went by his house a few times that month, checking first to see he wasn't working, but he was never home. Who could blame him? Living under a railway trestle would surely have offered more peace.

Then came the first day of class, and Peter wasn't there. He didn't show up on the second or third day, either. Mary was devastated. She thought he must have caved to his bully of a father. She planned to go around to his house that weekend to try to convince him to come back to school, to come back to Art class, or at the very least, to come back to her.

Instead, on Thursday, the RCMP knocked on the English room door and asked to see Mary. Mouths fell open as Mary paced to the front of the class and out into the hall, a tight fist of fear in her belly. Had she seen Peter? Did she know where he might be? Had he said anything lately to lead her to believe he might want to harm himself? Or anyone else for that matter? They didn't tell her much, only that he'd gone missing the night before and had left a note.

They found him in the river that afternoon, floating peacefully, face down in an eddy under a bank of swallow nests. The police gave the note back to his family and his father burned it before anyone else could read it, refusing to say what it contained.

September passed, and October did, too. Mary stopped painting. She handed in a few assignments at school but not many. Her marks plummeted below any hope of university entrance requirements. I let it go. What could I say? I figured she'd come around. Or maybe she'd need more time. It didn't matter to me.

One night, I got up out of bed and came downstairs to the kitchen to find her sitting in her housecoat simply staring at a lit candle, her face wet with tears. I sat at the end of the table, and with nothing of consequence to offer, simply reached out and put a hand on her shoulder. She shuddered. And without looking up, she said, "Why do people keep dying on me, Daddy?"

I dragged my chair around, pulled her by the arm into my lap, where we rocked and rocked and rocked. I had nothing to say.

But my Mary is a fighter. I went back upstairs to give her some peace. When I got up in the morning, her door was closed. I came downstairs and there on her easel was one blackbird lifting off from its perch on a fence post. The rising sun glittered in a river at the edge of the horizon. And in delicate silver letters over the whole image, as though painted on velum, were the words: "Dance for your life."

## ❧ *Thirteen*

EARLY ONE MORNING A FEW WEEKS LATER, THE DOOR OPENED to apartment 307. Randy put a coffee in Darren's hand and stepped past him into the entrance.

"Do you have a pair of decent boots?" Randy slurped at his coffee and wiped his mouth on the back of his sleeve.

"What time is it?" Darren asked, squinting through protesting eyes.

"Those'll do," Randy said, pushing aside the snakeskin and nodding toward the hiking shoes teetering on the edge of the shelf in the closet. "Put them on, and grab a vest. We're going out to further your education, son."

Randy took the back way to Len Rich's, partly to avoid some end of season construction on the highway, but mostly to impress upon Darren the expanse of land and history that lay beyond the town boundaries. The blind corners with their hidden sloughs lying in ambush; the wagon tracks grown over with clover and thistle, now camel-coloured and crispy in the gathering cold of October; the abandoned houses, each with a family name spread to the wind. All of this should have been frozen at this time of year, but the weather had been oddly warm the last few years, with twenty-degree days well into harvest. It made the mind dizzy.

Darren said nothing for the duration, glowering at his coffee and sitting silently behind gold-mirrored glasses. Randy guarded his own silence.

They pulled into the driveway and the truck coughed to a stop. Randy opened his door. "Aren't you going to ask what we're up to?"

Darren tipped his head from the window and looked over the top of his glasses. "I wasn't sure I wanted to know, but I figured I'd be a good Buddhist and believe all things would be revealed in time." He pulled on the handle to his own door. "I suppose the time is now, is it?"

"Tie up your boots," Randy said and hopped out. "You're a walking casualty."

Darren, to his credit, took two quick swallows of his coffee, set his paper cup on the dash, and double rabbit-eared the laces on his shoes.

Len Rich stepped off the veranda and limped across

the yard to greet his visitors. Darren stared at Len's leg with impropriety. Randy was about to elbow him when Len intervened.

"Never seen a war wound, son? I got myself a bum leg from going up against a horse with more will than me. It busted my knee in more places than the doctor could be bothered to count. If it'd been the other way 'round, they would have shot the horse, but I get along the best I can. With a little help now and then from your old man."

Darren and Randy looked at each other.

Len clapped Darren on the shoulder and led them toward the Quonset. "I don't suppose you've ever strung fence before, have you, son? What's your name, anyway?"

"Darren Boyce." The words came like ice grinding over gravel.

"Late night, eh?" Len laughed as the three entered the garage. "That's all right. A bit of fresh air will straighten you right up. You bring any work gloves? Thought not. Here." He lobbed a pair from the workbench, and Darren bent over to pick them up.

"Your old man is good to me, Darren. My wife gave me two beautiful daughters, but I never had any boys to help me out around the place — my father, God rest him, used to say two and ought — and Randy here was always only too glad to step in. He's a useful man, he is. Selfless. You'd do well to learn by him." He handed a shovel to Darren. "You take that to the green Ford. We'll stop at Grandad's section to fetch the posts. Randy, you help me with the wire. I've got it stashed in the back."

"Yes, sir," Randy said, rolling up his sleeves and searching for the lights.

"You guys want a cup of coffee or anything before we saddle up?"

"We're riding out?" asked Darren with something between fear and glee.

"It's a turn of phrase, boy," Len said, rolling his eyes. "Randy, where'd you dig up this kid?"

LEN HAD A FEW HUNDRED FEET OF FENCE OUT TO THE EAST that had come down last winter in a spectacular skidoo accident. The snow was deep and the night dark, and the driver both young and unfamiliar with the area. He'd gotten away with a few stitches and a paint job he'd be paying off to his father until well after he was legal to drive. It had taken Len all summer and more to get around to fixing it — with only one pair of hands, work could sometimes stretch beyond reason — and he'd managed by running his cattle on a neighbour's land. The men were getting older, and fewer and fewer of them bothered with livestock anymore, what with the massive operations down south, so it made the pastureland cheap to rent. But Len believed that renting undermines a man's sense of position, of responsibility, and the time had come to mend the fence. The posts were rotten anyway, Len said, ever the insufferable optimist.

Len's wealth was not obvious. His newest shirt had surely witnessed disco and the sexual revolution, but the land wealth he'd managed to keep intact would humble an oil baron. Although the dollar value for partially broken pasture land had hit an all-time low, Len still controlled a good hundred square miles of native short grass prairie, including a handsome grove of upland birch, the major portion of a tributary to the Red Deer River, an escaped plantation of lilacs and gooseberries, and the territories of several burrowing owls and swift fox. His management of the land — indeed, the very will to keep it together, unbroken — seemed backward to many people. And Len Rich didn't give a rat's ass. He had land enough to break your heart, Len did. It rolled away like sweet summer skin, curved and sloping under a golden yellow sheet.

The men pulled into an approach, then popped over the bank, along the narrow shoulder that separated the field's edge from the ditch. Even out here, refuse littered the sides of the road — a beer can shot nearly to bits, a rotten shoe, the better part of a fan belt. Darren bounced in his seat like a rookie horseman as Randy stretched his arms along the seat behind him.

Len stopped at one end of the broken section of fence, then opened the door of the truck and swung out in one fluid motion. He landed on his good leg and readjusted the cap on his head, then reached into his shirt for a plug of tobacco.

He offered the pouch to Darren, who grinned and shrugged, then picked up enough tobacco for two men and folded it under his bottom lip. Len slipped the pouch back in his shirt pocket and tried not to laugh. He walked around to the back of the truck and swung himself up into the pan, the world's most able-bodied lame cowboy.

"Darren," he said, rearranging his hat compulsively. "You can start hauling these fence posts up along the way. Just a few will do for now. We'll move the truck along as we go, eh?"

Darren opened his mouth to reply, but at the effort, his eyes squinted, his jaw quivered spasmodically, and a long thread of saliva leaked from his bottom lip. He shuddered, ever so slightly.

"You might want to take a smaller chaw next time. You took enough to last you a week. Put some of that in your pocket and save it for later."

Darren began to do as he was told, but Len hobbled over to the side of the pan and slapped the tobacco out of his hands.

"You shouldn't take everything so serious, son." He laughed. "I was just having one over on you. Pretty gullible for a so-called reporter. You never learned when people was lying?"

Len picked up a post in each hand and laid them in

Darren's arms like a sleeping baby. He added another three, and motioned Darren away. Then he pulled up his jeans around his knees and eased his backside down onto the gunnel of the truck. He waited until Darren was out of earshot.

"What's the story on him? You like him? Or did you bring him out here for me to make that decision for you?"

Randy smiled and kicked a boot up on the bumper. "Well, you're a pretty good judge of character, Len."

Darren had dumped off his last post and was returning to the truck.

"Sounds like you already made up your mind," Len said, smiling.

"Well, see, that's the thing. I doubt myself. I don't want to be one of these asshole fathers who believes no one could ever be good enough for his daughter. Mary's accused me of that, and I don't want to admit she might be right."

Randy rushed his last words out in a whisper as Darren approached, his nostrils flaring, and sweat glistening on his forehead.

"What's the matter, Darren? A strapping young man like you, winded? You sick?"

"No, Len. Just a little under the weather this morning is all. Randy caught me before I had time to freshen up."

"On the whiskey, eh? Well, that's all right, I suppose. Good to get it out of your system when you're young. How old are you, son?"

"Twenty-eight."

"Twenty-eight? A venerable old man. With a young thing like Mary?" He winked and jerked his head toward Randy. "You'd better watch your step and treat his baby right, you know. He'd turn you inside out with enough time left to weed the garden before supper." He managed to make it sound like a joke.

"I suppose we could all give Mary a little credit here and trust her good sense in people, eh?" Darren closed his eyes and pressed two fingers into each.

"Aw, don't worry about us, son. We're only making sure you're okay. There'll come a time in your life when you'll want to protect one of your own, and you'll understand. Randy, you take this wire, and Darren, grab the cutters and the wire stretcher. I suppose you've never done this before, eh?"

Darren looked over the top of his sunglasses wordlessly.

"All right. Crash course." Len swung down out of the truck and walked over to the first post. Darren followed.

"See where this here's broken?" he asked, bending down with a grunt for the loose end of the wire. "We're going to take these strands back to the post behind and wrap them around real good, then staple them a couple of times just to make sure they'll stay put. Then we're going to anchor a new piece of wire. Randy? Bring the roll, all right?"

Randy obliged. Len found the loose end and wheeled off a couple of loops. "Once we cut off the proper length, you're going to wrap this around the pole at the same height as the one you just tied off, then wrap it around the pole the same as you done the other one. Then it's over to the other end with the wire stretcher. This here." He held up a tangle of pulleys and rope, which Darren stared at sternly, like a doctor examining a wound.

"It'd help things immensely if you'd take off them ridiculous sunglasses." Len snatched them off Darren's face and folded them into his own pocket.

"Now. Pay attention. You'll want to know this. Two pulleys at one end. Two pulleys at the other. When I haul on the rope, that gives me an advantage of?"

Darren stared.

"Four. The fence has to be nice and tight, or else we'll have the cattle thinking it's a hammock. Once the wire is properly stretched, then we go along the pickets and staple on the wire. Right? Easy. My fences are four strand, all of them. The wire's fifty bucks a rod. That's sixteen and a half feet, if you didn't know. And as I was saying, the wire's expensive, but there's no use putting up a fence you can't trust. So they're all four strands. And I put my pickets twelve feet apart, instead of the regulation."

"Which is?"

"Well, a rod, naturally. What do they teach you in those city schools anyway?"

"Why do we need the posts?"

"Well, I figured while we was sprucing things up, we might as well replace the pickets. The old ones'll make good firewood for the Labour Day weekend, and the creosote in them will surely keep the flies down." He turned to Randy conspiratorially. "I like to a burn a tire once in awhile for that, too, but the wife goes snaky."

"How do we put them in?"

"The posts?"

"Yeah. Isn't there a machine for that?"

Len smiled. "Yes. It's called a strong back. A lot of fellas have those new hydraulic operations, but the day I start using one of them is the day I start wearing pyjamas in the afternoon and gumming my steaks. Here, let me show you."

He picked up the sledgehammer and knocked the old post back and forth a few times in its hole, then wrapped his two hands around it and pulled it out with a jerk. He stumbled slightly backwards, and Randy leaned against him without looking like he meant to. He grabbed the old man by the top of his arm. "Sorry, Len. Got in your way there."

"Randy, let go of me and let a foolish old man fall down if he has to." He smiled, then turned back to Darren. "Hold this," he said, tossing the post at him.

"Now. Getting the post into the ground in the first instance is a little tricky because the thing is six feet tall and looks me right in the eye. The easiest thing is for me to hold it in place, and you tap it in a few inches."

Darren looked at him warily and picked up the hammer. "What if I miss?"

"Then you have a bloody mess to clean up, and I don't say you'd have the stomach for that. So be careful, for God's sake."

Randy knew better than to offer to do it himself, and Len moved the post into place. He looked at Darren and nodded. Darren squared himself to the post and raised the hammer above his head.

"Be careful," Len warned him.

Darren let the hammer fall squarely on the head and the post sank easily. "A fine loam," Len said approvingly, getting out of the way. "Like a knife through butter. Good work. Now you only got another seventeen to go."

The three men spent the next two hours — possibly the hottest hours in October on record — taking out old posts, pounding in new ones, tightening, dropping and re-tightening wire. Darren cut his hand when he stretched the wire too tight, and buried a barb a little too close to home. But he worked hard, without much complaint, and despite the blood and sweat, seemed to brighten a bit throughout the morning. Randy was relieved that hard work seemed to suit him.

Back at Len's, they ate lunch on the veranda. Len's wife, Emma, had been watching them from the kitchen with binoculars (a little hobby of hers, being a birdwatcher, and having spent far too many hours alone) and had a shepherd's pie and biscuits ready to come out of the oven as they pulled up. When she served up three steaming plates full, taking nothing for herself, Len complimented her on her cooking. "It's enough to make grown men weep, honey."

They tore into the food like growing boys. Emma brought out glasses of iced tea and cleared away their plates and Len pushed his chair back from the card table and flopped his boots up on the railing. The air was still and filled with dust.

Darren sat with his arms folded, and soon his head was bobbing periodically as he lunged back from the brink of sleep.

"All that fresh air, eh, son? Why don't you go take a load off on the chesterfield?" Len jerked his head toward the living room, then stole a look at Randy. "I suppose he's allowed?"

"Free country." Randy shook his head slowly. "Although it's a shame to go wasting all this good company."

Darren pried his lazy eyelids apart. He wobbled dangerously as he stood from his chair, rattling it against the railing. He started toward the house, then changed his mind mid-step, and turned for the truck. He spilled himself over the seat and shut the door behind him.

Len pulled a jackknife from his back pocket, unfolded it and began picking at two bottom teeth. Randy watched with morbid interest, bracing for the blade to slip.

"I suppose you're waiting for my assessment, are you?"

Randy gave a self-effacing grunt. "I don't know. You have one to give?"

Len worked the blade up and down thoughtfully. "It's a shame what happened to that boy Peter there a few years back. I thought him and Mary were just about perfect for each other."

LATER THAT NIGHT, WHEN DARREN HAD REPAIRED TO RIVER-bend Estates and Randy was home alone, thunder roared over the mountains like a wall of water, and the silver air sang with the acid smell of lightning. Evening fell to night in a heartbeat. Randy had felt it coming in the afternoon. His flesh twitched with danger — an animal instinct — and then came the hail, pounding like fists on the earth. He sat at the kitchen table, his aching arms bare to the night, one sweating beer in his hand. The streets held their breath, all the dogs and birds hushed in wonder and self-preservation. Only the leaves that remained on the trees dared whisper.

A flash of lightning. A shape in the hallway.

He sat still and counted the beats before the crash, took a pull on his beer.

Another flash. The shape remained.

*"Why do people keep dying on me, Daddy?"*

He wiped at his face, wet with tears, and went to bed.

## ❧ *Fourteen*

MARY: PRESENT DAY

A DOG BARKED AND A CROW CAWED AND MARY STIRRED awake. She looked at the ceiling, focused, blinked. Darren had rolled away from her in the night and lay facing the other side of the room. She studied his back. His spine curved gently like a sloping string of pearls. His skin was a maze of freckles and scars. She wondered about the scars. Just above his waist on his right hip was a rose-coloured mole sprouting a single crinkled hair. She fingered it back and forth, but resisted the urge to yank it. She kissed him lightly on the shoulder blade and laid her hands over the sheet on her belly.

She was finished sleeping, but still tired from the night before. She had worked the three to eleven shift alone, then had spent another hour cleaning up and stocking shelves. She'd passed on a drink with Tina, hoping to spend a bit of time with Darren planning the trip to the mountains he'd promised they'd take before Christmas. But she'd come home to find him gone and the apartment in a state. She cleaned until around one, then fell into a fitful sleep until Darren crept in hours later.

The room still smelled of sex, and the November sun through the window was insistent. She slipped out from under the sheet and made her way to the kitchen.

The linoleum was cool on her feet and a sunbeam scattered through a half glass of water on the counter. She passed her hands through her hair, twisting it into a quick bun as the day began to open. She'd have a couple of quiet hours to herself before the neighbour kids came home for lunch and woke Darren to a cranky, groggy start.

She made some toast, poured a glass of milk and stood on one foot in the kitchen, heron-like, eating absent-mindedly.

She moved to the couch and pulled her sketchbook from the shelf. Her last entry was more than two months ago and the space since then filled her with a sense of inertia, of silence, like a mouth opening wordlessly miles below the sea. She took a deep breath and forced gentleness upon herself. She was in a state of flux, after all, and she needed some extra energy to change phase. Surely, at the age of twenty-two, she hadn't made her last painting. She'd stopped before and come back to it. Truth was, she couldn't live without it.

She interrogated her crowded, yapping mind for an image. She hadn't tried to focus in awhile, and every time she bumped into something she might use, her mind drifted to creative accounting — the contents of the fridge, the state of her unattended toenails, the snoring tangle of complications in the next room (not necessarily in that order) — and she had to nudge herself back toward the task at hand, fumbling.

She let down her bun and instead braided her hair in pigtails, then picked up her pencil again. Darren rustled in the sheets and she thought about crawling back in alongside him, of how much she loved waking to him looking at her, stroking her. However, given the smell of whiskey coming off him, this wasn't likely the morning for that.

Such a cruel passion was painting. For days at a time, images would come to her, unasked for. Strange eyes caught in a strobe of light. A crab emerging from a baby's shoe discarded on a beach. A man, upside-down, balanced on his outstretched tongue. Then, for weeks, it would all just leave her like a bored lover, alone and resentful.

Peter. How long had it been since she had thought about him? His tight black curls and his fine bony hands. The way he had found a person inside her and pressed her to canvas so she could never forget. His house where he was never enough. His patient witness. His broken heart.

The river. How they had walked there. How they had planted their footprints in the smooth sand, an impropriety, an indulgence. How they had once braided their footsteps with those of a tiny shorebird. How he'd chosen that to be the final place.

A braid. A rope. A rope binding her to Peter, to place, an invisible thread buried over by years of wind and wear, like burying a child's afterbirth to root him to his home in the hope he might one day defend it like his own flesh.

She set aside her sketchbook, feeling bold enough to begin with a new canvas. She went to the boot closet and moved aside various leather jackets and tools discarded from the trunk of Darren's Camaro and found a large wooden frame and a roll of canvas. She slid them both down gently, so as not to disrupt the sediment above.

Randy had built this stretcher according to a set of plans she'd given him. Three feet high by two feet wide, with struts in the corners and one by twos crossed in the middle for stability. She unrolled the canvas, cut a rough length and shoved the rest under the couch.

She anchored the canvas with a staple on the middle of one side, then another on the opposite side and back around again, as if tightening the lug nuts on a tire. With a set of pliers, she pulled the canvas as tight as she could without ripping it, adding more and more staples as she went. The pliers had been a gift from Darren after he'd seen the blisters over her knuckles from trying to stretch the canvas by hand. The bruise at the base of her thumb from the staple gun was bad enough, but at least for that, at the end of long days in the "studio" — that is, their living room — he could give her hand massages. Those massages very often ended in the bedroom.

When she finished the stapling, she went around again with a hammer, tapping as quietly as she could to smooth away the sharp bits. She hung the new canvas on a bare nail in the wall and chose a new brush, a short flat hog-hair. She stroked the perfect bristles, which bunched together neat as a laser's edge. It made her happy to be beginning. She often felt it was like sleeping with a new lover or visiting a new country.

This morning, though, as Mary stood poised in front, the blankness of the canvas was less inviting. It was solid ice to a diver trying to rise. It was an empty corridor after another wrong turn. It was a fork in the road, no signs and no map. She forced herself to concentrate on the fabric, to pull the image out of the weave.

There had been fights recently over space. Painting was messy business, and even though she worked in acrylics, there was the drying time to consider. She couldn't always put everything away. She'd told Darren there wasn't much she could do about it, that she came with *stuff*. After all, he had insisted on taking the second bedroom for his office. So she had compromised. Perhaps too much. Maybe that's why she hadn't been painting lately.

She stared into the canvas again, and tried to push every gossipy thought from her mind. She pulled her gaze into a smaller and smaller circle, until she was looking deep into the shaft of a single point of darkness, into the river, with the smell of the sand in the air, the heat of the summer on her arms, the buzz of grasshoppers near the willows — the willows and the bank swallows and that particular September afternoon — even the stifling stillness in the heart of the long grass, as though time had stopped and the oxygen was slowly burning away.

She blinked, then reached under the table for her box of paints. She uncapped a tube of cadmium orange and squeezed a long line onto her palette. Then another of cobalt, and still another of rose madder. She added a fourth of white, then squinted at the assembly and let them blend in her mind.

She dipped in a brush, looked again at the canvas and smeared an anchor of orange on the horizon. With a second brush, she added a dollop of white and with a delicate twirl of the fingers, twisted the colours into a screw. A sense of beauty in the touch.

As she pulled back to her palette, her elbow brushed against the edge of the card table, and sent a jar full of up-ended paintbrushes flying into the coffee table with a crash.

Shards of glass exploded across the wood floor like a dollop of mercury.

Her shoulders slumped, irritated more by the delay than the mess. She stood to sweep up the mess and lowered one bare foot directly on a tiny glass assassin. She let go an involuntary yelp, then covered her mouth with her hands. She sat down again and pulled the splinter from the ball of her foot, licked her thumb and ran it over the bead of blood, which swelled again instantly.

There was a sound from the bedroom like a moan, the creaking of the mattress, footsteps on the carpet, then silence. Mary swivelled around on her chair and faced Darren with a small smile.

He did not return it. "What are you doing?"

A cloud across the sun of Mary. "What does it look like?"

"Couldn't it wait until a reasonable hour?" He was unshaven and his hair stood in shock atop his head.

"It's ten o'clock. I've been up for an hour, most of the neighbours are at work. It seems perfectly reasonable to me."

Nothing.

"Darren, it's my painting. I have to do it somewhere. I haven't done it in so long. And I had an idea this morning. It's a rope. Three sets of footprints at the river. You know, in the sand. Down by—" She lost steam. She'd never told him about Peter. Besides, Darren was clearly not interested in her internal creative dialogue this morning. "Are you hungover?"

"Yes."

Mary looked at her bare feet and curled her big toes at their knuckles. She felt restless and somehow guilty under his gaze.

"We share this space," she attempted. She was nervous, like a gambler placing a bet she can't afford.

"Precisely. So why don't you have a little respect?" Darren continued to stare at her, through her, then went back to bed without a word.

Mary left the glass shards where they were, left the paint sliding toward the floor, slipped on a long-sleeved shirt and went out for a walk.

"SO THEN I SAID, 'BUT OFFICER, MY ZEBRA HAS A BUM KNEE.'"

Mary blinked and turned toward Sara. "What?"

"Hello, Space Girl. Where have you been today? I don't think you heard a word I said. You just missed some very important information about my mother and her boyfriend's sex life." Sara pulled her store jacket closed and folded her arms in a vaguely threatening gesture.

"Sorry," Mary said. "Information I'll no doubt be unable to live without. Start again?"

"Just kidding. What's up?"

Mary considered her answer, defensive over Sara's concern. "Oh, I don't know. Darren was a little weird yesterday morning. It's no big deal, though. I'm just feeling a little low today." She turned away behind the counter, and began straightening the stacks of paper bags.

"Hold on." Sara paused. "What do you mean, weird?"

Mary's chest tightened. "It's no big deal. He was just a bit hungover and cranky, that's all. I was making noise in the house and I woke him up. He'd only had a few hours' sleep."

"It's your house, too. What kind of noise were you making?" Sara planted her hands on her hips. "Mary Thompson, were you sanding down the kitchen floor again?"

Mary was not in the mood. "I was just setting up for a painting. My card table came apart, and it woke him up."

Sara was scandalized. "Occupational hazard, Mary."

"Not to someone who reeks of booze at ten in the morning."

"Well, that's his problem, isn't it? What did he say to you?"

"Sara, I —"

"What did he say to you?"

Mary threw her head back and shook her hair down over her shoulders. "Nothing, really." She heard herself being defensive, and softened. "It was more the way he looked at me. Like I was unwelcome. It was cold."

"Unwelcome? Jesus. Has he brought in a dime since he's been living here? He's sponging off you and your old man. He's shameless and lazy."

"Well, it's taking him some time —"

"Oh, no you don't. You don't really believe that anymore, do you? I can see now why he got fired."

Mary lacked the energy to find a comeback. She blinked heavily.

"And where does he get off telling you to stop painting? Darren used to bring the art out in you, didn't he? And now he's nailing it shut inside." Sara paused. "What does that tell you?"

Mary tucked her hair behind her ear and ran her hands over the flat of her stomach, picking at lint on her shirt.

After a minute, Sara changed the subject. Her voice was gentle. "Ned's getting a karaoke machine down at the bar tonight and Tina will be working. Let's go."

"I don't —"

"No arguments. Just nod." Sara cupped Mary's ears in her hands and tipped her head back and forth.

Mary smiled. Sara grabbed a sucker from the bucket their boss kept for kids near the cash register, winked at Mary and breezed out the door for lunch, leaving the frantic bells to their gossip.

NED, THE BAR OWNER, WAS BENT OVER THE KARAOKE machine. Brawny arm on brawny knee, he squinted at the control panel as if the instructions were printed in hieroglyphics. He found the power switch, flipped it on and plugged in the microphone with a crackle that could have set a deaf man on edge. He lurched upright with an asthmatic gasp and flipped the television to channel three for the lyrics. There was no messing around with Ned: karaoke was to be done in style.

He entered a string of numbers to let a few songs roll out like wallpaper. "*Oooh, baby, baby, it's a wild world. It's hard to get by with just one smile.*"

Ned moved across the dance floor to the bar with steps that were a cross of mambo and waltz, came around behind and grabbed a generic "Beer" beer from the cooler.

"I can't believe you carry that stuff," Tina said, pointing to the black-and-yellow label. "Nobody orders it. And it's 'just upon a smile,' not 'with just one smile'."

"Suddenly I have the grammar police working behind the bar. And about the beer, it's fine that nobody else orders it. All the more for me."

"You own the joint. Shouldn't you be drinking Lagavulin or something?"

"My dear, such extravagant tastes do not make for good financial returns. I'm going to have to cut you out of my will."

"Damn, and here I was, planning to spend my old age reigning over The Derrick House. Whatever will I do?" Tina flipped her palms upward and a lock of hair fell into her eyes. She turned toward Mary, who had appeared in the door, and waved her in impatiently.

Ned came around the bar and wrapped Mary in a smothering hug. "It's about time you showed up here, Mary. Where've you been, darling?"

Mary planted her chin on Ned's shoulder and patted his back. "Good to see you, too, Ned. But if you don't let go of me, I'll have you charged." She stood back from him at arm's length and smiled. "Nothing personal. Just been busy is all."

Ned shot a knowing look at Tina, a look full of scandal and titillation. "Yes, having a man takes it out of you, doesn't it?"

"I ought to stay away more often, if this is the kind of welcome I get," Mary said, ruefully. "Ned, I see you've spared no expense again for the karaoke machine."

"I'm a connoisseur, what can I say? Besides, we knew you were coming."

Mary coughed nervously and looked at Ned as if he'd caught her in her underwear. "I don't know. I'm a little rusty."

"Don't lie to me, Mary Thompson. We all know if you were gagged and buried in sand, you'd still sing like a mockingbird. Don't go getting on your high horse about karaoke, Missy. God gave us throats so we could laugh as well as sing. Now give us your coat," he said, slipping it off her shoulders, "and let's get you a drink. How about a margarita to go with your lovely aprés-summer look this evening?" He stopped and looked at her, made a kissy face and stepped behind the bar. He balled up her coat and tossed it on a shelf under the counter.

"A margarita?" She was skeptical. It felt like ordering cappuccino in a gas station.

"Well, tequila and lime Tang in a salty glass," Tina said. "It's our own little rendition. Consider it the karaoke of cocktails."

Ned snapped a dishtowel at Tina. "That's enough out of you. You'll scare away the customer." He looked to the corner table, where a lone man sat. "I mean, *customers*."

Ned salted the rim of a nearly forgotten martini glass, cracked in two ice cubes from a metal tray, added two shots of gold tequila, and splashed in a toxic-looking green liquid. He slid it across the counter to Mary. "There's no charge for that," he said. "I'm trying out a new recipe."

Mary sat up on the stool and cupped the drink in two hands. She peered over the rim of the glass and saw her reflection.

"It looks like dye for some kind of heart test." She looked up. Ned did not respond. She took a sip. It tasted like salty tequila and lime Tang. She shivered a little, from the salt, or the cold, or the God-knows-what.

"Well?" Ned nodded encouragingly.

Mary nodded after a time. "Well, yeah. Needs some work. Crushed ice. You might want to try crushed ice. And maybe some freshly squeezed lime juice."

"My dear, I'll agree there's something to be said for doing things properly. But the clientele around here wouldn't know freshly squeezed lime juice if it kicked them in the shins. In fact, they'd probably complain it wasn't real Tang. But crushed ice — now there's an idea. I could get one of them snow cone machines. It'd be like one of those blend-your-own soft serve set-ups. We could have margaritas in twenty-four flavours. Chocolate margaritas. Imagine. They do it for martinis. Why not margaritas?"

"I think tequila and chocolate syrup might make uncomfortable bedfellows." Mary shivered again, taking another crack at her drink.

The last song ended on the karaoke machine. Mary looked at Tina, who jerked her head in the direction of the machine. Well, thought Mary, at least it was a chance to get away from her drink. She hopped off the chair and smoothed her skirt.

"Now there's a girl. Are you taking requests? Do 'La Bamba' and we'll turn off the screen and guess at the words. That was a national pastime for about a week there in 1990."

"How about some Cyndi Lauper? 'Time After Time.' Before Cyndi, I didn't know you could rhyme 'time' with 'going'."

Tina shrugged. Mary picked up a binder full of songs, scanned down the first list, flipped the page, then stopped. She plugged in the number, picked up the microphone and waiting for the song to load.

A lazy snare drum limped out of the speakers, followed

by a muffled slide guitar. Mary laughed nervously, scanned the bar for witnesses, shook her hair in ripples down her back, waited for, then missed her cue. To jeers and heckles from the bar, she reset the song.

"*The sun comes up, it's Tuesday morning ...*" Enthusiastic cheers.

"*... looks me right in the eye, guess you forgot to close the blind last night ...*" Ned flipped open his lighter, and Tina leaned over the bar, with her chin in her hands.

Mary eased through the song like a long body stretching in the sun, gentle, yet full of conviction. Then she returned to the bar with enough courage to tackle her margarita.

"You started the party without me!" Sara walked through the door, a pout on her lips and a young man in a cowboy hat and slippery boots in tow. Near the pillar in the dance floor, his feet shot apart as if propelled by magnets. But he quickly righted himself and smirked at the people staring.

"Sand. It keeps the dance floor cooperative," Ned offered. "But it's a bitch on the heels."

"Who's your goofy friend, Sara?" Tina asked.

"She means that in the best possible way," Mary added to the goofy friend.

"This here's my cousin Wade. He was on his way through to Edmonton. Stopped in for a visit." She patted his arm.

Sara turned to Mary and Tina. "We heard there was

karaoke tonight, and that we might have some heavyweight local talent showing up, so we thought we might mosey down." She dropped Wade's arm. "Wade's got a set of pipes on him, too. Could we have two whiskeys, Tina?"

"May I recommend the margaritas?" Tina faked her obligatory brightness, then screwed up her face and pointed to Mary's drink.

"Yeah, right. I've heard about them."

"I'll try one," Wade ventured.

"All right," Tina nodded appreciatively. "And you, Sara?"

Sara shook her head. Mary mouthed the words, *Good move.*

Wade pulled off his hat and winked at Ned. Underneath, he was well-scrubbed as a young boy at a Christmas concert. The five of them sat up at the bar and proceeded to drink.

NOW MISTER, THE DAY MY NUMBER COMES IN,
*I ain't never gonna ride in no used car again.*

Wade put down the microphone and skidded across the dance floor back to the bar.

"I love that song," Mary said, her head bobbing up and down from where her chin rested on her folded arms.

"Me, too," Wade said, settling himself again on his stool. "I was so glad to discover that Springsteen was a folksinger."

Mary looked at Tina, then back at Wade as if he were a dangerous thing.

Wade was confused. "Well, it's not a blinding insight, I suppose, but —"

Tina patted him on the arm and shushed him.

"No, you're right." Mary said, cutting the tension. "And he's got the arms for it too, eh? He looks more like a mechanic than a rock star. It makes me respect him more as a musician."

An uncomfortable silence swelled among them. Ned shook his head, grabbed his drink and hustled — in his fashion — over to the karaoke machine. He programmed a number and smoothed his hair as he waited for the first notes of the song.

An electrical buzz, a click, then an almost panicked waltz twisted from the speakers.

*If you were the woman, and I was the man. Would I send you yellow roses, would I dare to kiss your hand?*

The audience at the bar shook with relieved laughter.

"It's not your typical karaoke reportoire, is it?" Sara offered.

"He's got a friend in Calgary who does them up on a two-hundred-dollar keyboard and a drum machine. It's great. It's like some kind of secret karaoke society. Don't ever tease him about it."

"Vicious about it, is he?" Wade joked.

Tina rocked her head from side to side. "Well, yeah. He

firmly believes in every human being's right and ability to sing."

"It's not just music, it's democracy!" Sara pointed to the ceiling dramatically.

"Yeah, only he would say it the other way around," Mary said, and got off her stool to hug Ned as he returned to the bar. Tina took his glass and topped up his margarita.

"This is great, Ned," Wade said, leaning across the bar to shake his hand.

Ned caught his breath, took his glass from Tina and wiped the shine from his forehead. "You're damned right. Low-brow entertainment is the best. Always."

"More democratic," Wade offered, grinning.

"Precisely," Ned said with an emphatic shrug, splashing a healthy portion of his margarita to the floor. "Oh, look at me. These go straight to my head. You'll do," he said. "You'll do." Then he sat down, glowing like a proud father.

Mary felt light for the first time in weeks, as though her very bones might break from the velocity of her happiness.

There was a bang, and all five heads snapped to the corner table. The salesman had passed out, knocking his beer to the floor, where froth poured from the bottle like a lazy river flowing. Wade and Tina rushed to help him, while Ned rifled around for a key to a room upstairs. He lobbed it at Tina, while Wade threw the man over his shoulder, and the two went upstairs to deposit him.

"I guess that's one more highway in want of Amway cleaning products tomorrow," Sara said, stirring her whiskey with her finger.

Mary smiled, the warmth of silly laughter spreading delicate wings in her heart.

"Having a good time?"

Mary turned to see Darren standing in the door. The wings folded, her heart crumpled. He walked toward her stool, took her gently by the arm and led her toward the men's bathroom.

Sara and Tina made to follow, but Ned stopped them.

In the bathroom, Darren stopped and turned toward Mary. He took her face in his hands and rested his forehead against hers. "I was looking for you," he said. "I'm sorry about yesterday. I was an asshole. Come home with me."

"Oh, but Darren, I'm having a really good time. I haven't been out in a long time. I just realized I miss my friends."

"I miss you, too." He looked and looked until his blue eyes could melt butter. "Things have been kind of shitty between us lately."

His unexpected tenderness stopped her. Her throat began to itch.

"Come home with me," he asked again. "Please?"

They returned to the bar where Mary retrieved her thin jacket and slid under Darren's ropy arm. Ned cleared his throat and Wade waved.

THEY LAY NAKED ON THE GREEN VELVET COUCH, MARY'S HAIR spread around like a cloudy river delta, their clothes in an urgent heap on the floor. They were resting, Mary on Darren's shoulder, and his finger tracing round and round her navel.

"Who was that guy at the bar?" he asked.

"Who? That salesman?" Mary held a length of hair to the light and inspected the ends for splits.

"No. That one who seemed to have your undivided attention."

"Oh. I wouldn't say that. His name's Wade."

"Who is he?"

"Why? Are you jealous?"

"Could be." Darren dug his forefinger nail into her belly ever so slightly. She grabbed his hand and pulled it away.

"He's a cousin of Sara's. I'd never met him before."

"Did you find him attractive?"

"I don't know. I suppose." She lifted her head from his shoulder and craned to look at him. Then she lay back again. "Don't worry. No one could take the place of Darren Boyce. You wouldn't let them."

"That's right. And you ain't seen nothing yet, baby." He reached down and lifted her chin again. He looked into her eyes and his lips stretched into something resembling a smile.

She squinted and laughed half a laugh. "Okay, Captain Ominous. I have to pee. Let me go before I make a mess on the floor."

The whiskey on him was rank. He tightened his grip.

"Funny." She tried to twist her wrist in his hand, but she couldn't move. "Let me go."

A terrible silence. The moon glinting off his bare chest. Cold settling around her heart.

"Darren. You're scaring me. Let me go."

"Don't be scared, little Mary. I won't hurt you. If you don't make me. You don't want to make me hurt you, do you?"

Sweat beaded at the back of her neck and her throat tightened. Her eyes darted around the room involuntarily, looking for escape.

"Mary. The best thing for you to do is relax. We're just having a little chat here. It's good to chat, don't you think? Or am I only a good lay to you? Women these days." Darren rolled his eyes mawkishly.

She blinked away the tears gathering in her eyes, and stared at him. He drew his face near to hers again and kissed the air in front of her lips.

Then he dropped her hand and twisted himself on top of her in a mad fit of tickling.

She rolled out from underneath him and wiped at her eyes. Fresh gulps of air scraped at her lungs. She felt around her wrist. "Jesus, Darren. You nearly gave me a stroke. And broke my arm to boot. You scared the hell out of me."

He leaned forward and kissed her forehead. "I'm sorry,

baby. I was just having a laugh. I didn't mean to scare you. You know I would never hurt you."

Mary walked to the bathroom, watching over her shoulder as she went.

## ⁊ *Fifteen*

WHAT CAN A PERSON SAY ABOUT CHRISTMAS? A GIRL AND HER dad. The presents. The tree. The cousins and snow and candy and meals in perpetuity and everything else everyone secretly hopes for and dreads. We had it all. And Christmas Day just for us. I'd lie in bed in the morning until she'd come to my bedside and lean over my face to see if I was awake. "Daddy?" she'd whisper. "Are you awake? *Santa came last night,*" she'd say as though secretly fearing that some year he might not come, and that this might have been the one.

One year stands out, though, and it's important because if ever there was a time when my little girl showed me the breadth and depth of her heart, this was it.

It was Boxing Day, and Mary was twelve, I'd say. Against my better judgement, I decided we'd go into Red Deer and check out the madness at The Bay. Brenda had bought me a pair of pants suitable for wearing at my next golf game with our MLA, which might happen right after I turned the roof and sod and started a cottage goat-cheese business, so I had those to return. And Mary had some Christmas money she thought she could use to buy some new watercolour brushes. We parked several blocks away for a quick getaway and jogged through the bitter cold straight to the front door, banging our shoes on the rubber entrance mat. She was old enough to handle herself in the store on her own, so I told her I'd meet her back at the entrance in half an hour, and that we'd go somewhere for lunch after that.

The lineup at the men's counter was mercifully short, and it took me only a few minutes to exchange the khakis for a respectable sweatshirt. I had plenty of time left before we were to meet, I wandered over to the craft counter where I thought Mary might be appearing presently.

She, too, had already found what she needed, and was first in line behind a little boy at the counter. But something curious was happening, so I hung back to watch.

The boy, barely big enough to see over the counter, was on his tiptoes, counting through a large drift of coins. To the side sat a small, shiny cardboard box. Some kind of toy, images of which had undoubtedly pummelled him from catalogues and TV since Halloween. He counted the coins painstakingly, pushing them into piles, and when he thought he'd made a dollar, inched them over toward the cashier, who would count them again and push some back, or take more from the shrinking pile. It was excruciating to watch. At times the boy's legs would tire and he would have to flatten his feet. Then he'd take a breath and muster up the courage to start again. Or he'd put his hands in his pockets for a moment, turn his head behind him to Mary, who would politely turn her own so as not to embarrass him. The sleeve of his coat was torn, and he wore only canvas shoes despite the deep snow outside. He had no hat and the tips of his ears were burning — from shame or from the recent cold, it was impossible to know.

The cashier looked down over her reading glasses and over the edge of the counter. "Son, we'll have to finish up here, there are other people waiting."

Up he came on his toes again for the final stretch. Seven piles sat before the cashier. He counted out the last of his coins. Seven dollars and forty-two cents. The box, whatever it held, apparently cost more than that. The boy stared at the cashier, apparently begging her understanding. She shook her head. They looked at each other. And in a moment that for her would surely pass at the end of the day, he felt the full weight of poverty. The want, the shame, a head shaking *no* in a sea of plenty. This was where wars started. The boy would remember this. The cashier swept the coins into a new white plastic bag and handed it to him. He slipped it into his pants pocket, left the cardboard box where it lay and walked away.

Mary stared. First at the cashier, then at the little boy whose pace was picking up as his anger mounted. She seemed stuck in her place. Then she stepped forward to the counter, lay down her brushes, passed over her ten-dollar bill, but instead bought the shiny little box. She pocketed the change, grabbed the receipt and ran after the little boy, who was just about to step back out into the cold.

She tapped him on the shoulder. "Hey, uh, hi. I saw you at the counter back there."

"Well?" His eyes were red where he'd smeared away the tears.

"Well, uh, I saw you were going to buy this, uh —" she looked at the box to see what it was, "this Power Ranger, and well, I got two this year, so why don't you take mine?" She held out the box in her hand.

He looked at the box, then at her, scowling. "What's a girl doing getting a Power Ranger for Christmas?"

"I know. Stupid, isn't it? Can't help it. Never was much into Barbies." She held out her hand again. "Take it. I was just going to return it."

"Well, why don't you?"

"Uh —" she stalled. She hadn't thought about this one.

"They, uh, only let you return so many things at this store. I gotta save some of my returns for my birthday because people always buy me stuff I don't like then." She was a terrible liar, thankfully.

The boy looked at her. He probably didn't believe her either. But he wanted that Power Ranger and this was his chance. "Okay." He took the box and turned it over in his hands a few times. He started to walk away, too embarrassed to say anything further. Then he stopped, turned around and started to pull the bag of coins out of his pocket. Mary saw what he was up to and made for a quick escape.

"Okay, thanks. I gotta go do some more stuff. See ya." She turned on her heels and trotted back to the counter.

She reached in her pocket and counted her change. One dollar and twenty-seven cents. Each brush she had intended to buy was three dollars. She put the bill and the coins back in her pocket and, making sure the boy was out of sight, turned back for the exit.

I was stunned by what I had just seen. I let a few minutes pass, so as to not blow her cover, then came at the doors from the other side.

"Hi, honey," I said, and kissed the top of her head. "I got rid of those pants. See what I got?" I held open the bag for her approval.

"Nice."

"Did you get your brushes?" I asked, opening the door

for her to tell me her version of what I'd just watched.

"No." She put her hands in her pockets and looked away. "They didn't have the ones I wanted. I think I'll just put the money in the bank for now. Are we still going for lunch?" She slyly changed the subject. "Can we go to that place on the hill that makes the really good milkshakes?"

Not bad, if I do say so myself.

## ❧ Sixteen

ON THE TWENTY-NINTH OF DECEMBER, DARREN SAT IN A COR-
ner booth at a roadside diner near Brooks, fiddling with a silver napkin box. Through the greasy ovals of fingerprints
(forensic evidence from highway fugitives, lovers on the run,
lonely salesmen) he peered at his foggy reflection. His brown
eyes tipped toward his ears, giving his face the suggestion of
a wince, and his ever-shifting sideburns were now cropped
close and short. He fixed the collar of his shirt under his
sweater, and pulled his yellow acrylic scarf tighter around his
neck. Outside, where the Christmas lights blinked in the
premature darkness, was the kind of cold that slammed your

nostrils shut like a valve. Here in the stuffy diner he was lapping up the heat.

The waitress delivered a coffee and left without taking his order. Tightness spread through his chest, and he stopped himself from yelling after her.

He rolled the plastic menu into a tube and looked at his watch. Four fifty-six. It was a three-hour drive home, and he was hungry. Mary would be expecting him for supper. The thought of her bent at the stove with leftover turkey like somebody's mother, desperate to please, made the room loom large and swallow him whole. Bound and gagged with domesticity. His ears rang.

"— comes with a side salad and fries, for eight ninety-nine." The waitress inspected the edges of her pad and stood silently.

Darren looked up the length of her, the little roll over the belt of her apron, the elegant curve to her elbow, the snarl of hangnails around her bitten fingernails, the words printed across her breasts: I-N-D-I-A-N-A H-O-O-S-I-E-R, the eyeliner bleeding from her lower lids, the long white line of scalp dividing her braided ponytails that cleaved her head into perfect halves. She sucked her top lip through her bottom teeth.

He realized she was waiting for him to order.

"That's fine," he said, clearing his throat.

"How do you want it?" She chased her pencil around the word "special."

"Excuse me?"

"Your steak?" She bent down closer to his ear and lowered her voice. He caught a whiff of patchouli, sweat and fryer grease. "Given the state of the kitchen, I'd recommend well done."

"Oh," he said, tearing his eyes away from her breasts and raising them to her eyes. "Yeah," he said. "Well done."

"WE SHOULD CRACK THE WINDOW," THE WAITRESS SUGgested, tracing her finger up Darren's breastbone.

"But it's colder than a witch's titty out there," he said, propping himself up on an elbow to peer out the back seat window. The fog on the windows was starting to melt into long, thin worms wriggling into the cracks of the upholstery.

His movement nearly rolled her off the edge of the seat. She flung an arm around his waist to keep herself propped up. "I know, but if we don't get some air in here we're going to die of asphyxiation."

Darren looked at her, the hint of a snarl on his lips.

"It happens," she said defensively.

"I know it happens. It's just an awfully big word for a waitress, isn't it?" He swept a lock of hair away from her jaw and tried to poke it back into one of her ponytails.

She pulled her lips across her teeth in a tight facsimile

of a smile. "They like us waitresses to have a vocabulary. Helps us get along with our customers."

"And get off with them." He reached around behind her and cupped a cheek.

"That has nothing to do with vocabulary. I believe our conversation was 'What?', 'Well done,' 'When?', 'Now?', 'Here?', 'Okay.' And now you've made a wicked woman out of me in the back seat of your Camaro."

"Right. This is a new experience for you, is it?"

"Utterly."

Darren looked at her, amused.

"Well. Brooks is a little slow. We all need our hobbies."

He reached down for his shirt, and passed her hers. With a series of grunting contortions, they each got partially dressed, then lay back to catch their breath. Darren looked at the girl. "I envy you, you know?"

She flicked her braids over her shoulders and arched her back, smoothing her shirt over her breasts, admiring the line of her own ribs. "Why?" she asked, distractedly.

"The people you meet. All those strangers and you, thrown together with the mutual goal of comfort. I'll bet you rarely even find out their names. But if they're just stopping through town, you become their memory of this place. You must *be* Brooks to many people. The dramas you get to be part of. Hell, you even get laid."

"I suppose. But you make it sound like missionary work.

I'm slinging all-day breakfasts, not curing leprosy. You haven't been out from under your rock very much lately, have you?" she asked, still absorbed in her own body. "What do you do for a living?"

"I'm a journalist."

"Well, there you go. You must meet a lot of interesting people," she said, folding her arms behind her head and inspecting the roof.

"Used to. I haven't been working much lately. But even when I was, it wasn't the same thing as what you get to do. I had to ask all the tedious questions, find out what was really happening — or at least what they wanted you to think was really happening. And I had to care. You don't have to do any of that stuff. You get to make it all up."

"Brooks is slow. But not that slow. If I want stories, I turn on the TV." Suddenly bored and ready to leave, she inched her legs around and rolled over him to grab her underwear from out of the back window. She wriggled into them, taking care not to bang her head on the overhead light. She stepped into her boots, checked her eye makeup in the rear-view mirror, smoothed the stray hairs around her face. Then she turned to Darren and gave him a quick kiss on the cheek.

"Look me up if you're ever back this way again. We're a very hospitable crowd."

Slamming the car door behind her, she hustled across

the parking lot, struggling against the wind to get her arms through the sleeve of her coat. At the restaurant door, she turned and waved. Then she was gone.

Darren pulled on the rest of his clothes and barrel-rolled over the front seat of the car to the driver's side, put the car in gear and pulled away for home.

THERE WAS NO LIGHT ON IN THE WINDOW WHEN DARREN pulled up to the apartment building in Juniper Butte. Even the Christmas tree was unplugged. It was eleven o'clock, dark, and the wind whined. He turned the key and the car rumbled to a stop. In the dying musty breath of the car heater, he shuddered and braced himself against the coming cold. Through the double beams of the headlights, snow swirled like a million starlings dipping and soaring on the whim of the wind, rushing the lights wide-eyed and angry. He turned off the lights and sat for awhile, watching as his eyes grew accustomed to the night and objects emerged from the darkness. A fire hydrant, sulking darkly grey under the starless night. A tree, lashed and stripped under the charge of winter. The big black creepy dumpster in the corner of the parking lot.

Which reminded him.

He flicked on the interior light and kneeled up on the front seat, groping around behind for a cold, greasy lump of evidence. He found it tucked in between the leather halves of the seat, located the round rubber ring and extracted it carefully. He tied the neck of the condom, wiped his fingers unceremoniously on the thighs of his jeans and grabbed his coat. He slammed the car door behind him, and flicked the thing into the dumpster as he jogged across the asphalt, into the echoing stillness of the building's stairwell and up the metal stairs to number 307.

The door was locked. He fished around for the key, let himself in, and switched on the lamp over the table.

In the centre of the table sat a large homemade pizza decked out with leftover turkey and olives and artichokes and capers and cheese that didn't melt in the baking and whole tiny fish who'd lost their eyes to salt: to Darren, the thing looked like a bad joke. A single slice was missing. Beside that stood a single carnation in a chipped beer stein. Two place mats. Two napkins. Two plates, a dusting of crumbs on one of them.

He threw his keys on the table, pried off his shoes with his toes, and looked around the freshly tidied room. In the corner on top of a speaker sat a tiny clay pot: the cactus he'd brought home for Mary from the badlands. He walked over and picked it up, the cold from the glass of the patio door sweeping his skin. The bloom was long since gone and the turgid green leaves had withered, collected a dusting of white. The pot was white with salt, and the soil was wet. He returned it to its place with a faint sneer.

In the corner, the tree stood watching him. A few pieces

of tinsel twisted in an unseen breeze, and the angel, fashioned from a paper-towel roll, ribbons and crepe, nodded at the floor and averted her eyes. He felt his way past the kitchen. He should at least make a show of eating some pizza, but the steak he'd had in Brooks was still heavy in his gullet, and besides, a whole pizza made from things pulled from brine? It offended his redneck inclinations and gave him a craving for deer sausage. He made his way to the bathroom, where he brushed his teeth and took a long piss, all in the dark.

He'd become used to late nights and now it seemed too early to go to bed, but he didn't care. Mary must be out. She would come home and find him safely sleeping away in their little cocoon, and think he'd had a hard day. It would spare him the drama about missing supper. Perfect.

He pulled off his clothes except for his undershirt and kicked them into a corner of the bathroom, hunkering like a mangy stray. He padded to the bedroom, a king in his kingdom, his prick bouncing breezily.

The lamp switched on as he came through the door of the room.

"Oh," he said, startling a little. "You're home. I figured you were out with the girls."

Mary rolled over under the sheets and looked at him without expression. "Where were you?"

"Tired? After a long day of hard labour at the IGA, huh?"

He slid between the sheets and wrapped his arm around her waist, deliberately touching his cold feet to her legs. She flinched. "Hearing about the body fluids of old ladies and ringing in their boxes of tissues all day? I can see how you'd be beat out." He laughed at his own joke and pulled himself closer to her.

"Someone's got to pay the rent. Where were you?" she asked again.

"I told you before. I went to see a man about a horse." He laughed again. Then he relented. "I went to see Chris about the project. There's no money happening yet, but that's no reason not to start kicking around ideas. Book design. You know, dust-cover bios and things like that."

"You're a man before your time. How about writing the thing first?"

"I'm working on it. But the whole thing has got to be a collaboration, so Chris and I have to be on the same page."

"And?"

"It went really well. I gave Chris Grandma's diary so he could think about places to shoot. He's got some great ideas already and his sense of composition is very lyrical. I think it will be great. We scoped out some locations today."

"Bit hard in the snow, wasn't it?"

"Well, we just stuck to the main roads. This will have to be a summer project anyway — the prairies are best captured in the summer, I think. All this work will have to be repeated in May or June. But it's good to start drawing the map."

Mary rolled over and looked him in the face. "Chris called here today and left a message saying he had to cancel."

"Oh."

Darren's mouth opened once or twice, like that of an actor stammering in a silent film. But he said nothing more. She rolled over and switched off the lamp, removing his arm from her waist as she did so.

He lay without moving in the darkness for a time until his breathing evened. She rolled back toward him and studied his face: the lines around his slack mouth, parted slightly with exhaustion; the stray unruly hairs in his eyebrows that gave him an unwashed look even at the height of spit and polish; his high, smooth forehead, unworried in the arms of sleep.

He smelled funny. Stale and unwashed. Musty.

He smelled of sex.

Mary closed her eyes and felt her heart quicken as suspicion washed over her. She held her breath. She exhaled. She held her breath again. She hated the man beside her. Wanted him to wake and tell her it wasn't true. No, she wanted him to *prove* it wasn't true; she was tired of being told things she had no choice in believing. Tired of complying with ignorance.

She rolled gently out of bed and tucked the quilt tightly in beside him. She pulled her jeans from the wooden chair in the corner, where they lay with attitude, and buttoned them over her pyjama bottoms. She tiptoed out of the room and closed the door soundlessly behind. In the kitchen, she found the keys to Darren's car, slipped her bare feet into a pair of ski-doo boots, and hauled on a sweatshirt and a parka over her T-shirt. She clumped down the metal stairwell — her footfall matching Darren's of only an hour before — and out into the parking lot. She opened up the Camaro, slipped into the front seat and slammed the door behind her.

She rubbed her hands: a frigid night. She wasn't sure what she was doing here in the car. She looked around, over the front seats, running her hands over the cracked white leather. She opened up the glove compartment and peeked in between the papers, the manuals, the spent pens and dirty plastic forks. She pulled out the ashtray and poked through the ashes. She sat for a moment feeling foolish for digging through the pocket lint of Darren's life like this, foolish about what she'd been reduced to. She considered throwing a rock through their bedroom window and taking off with his car. Instead, she opened the door and hustled around into the back seat, still unsure of what she was hoping to find.

And there it was.

A tiny plastic wrapper, torn in half and winking in the amber street light, *Sheik* written in a slanted font atop a purple band that read: THIN. She leaned down close to the floor and poked at it with her finger, as though it were a deadly tropical insect presumed dead. It flipped dutifully onto its back. *Lubricated. Effective against pregnancy,* HIV *(*AIDS*) and* STDs.

The bastard.

She sat back in the seat with her ears ringing. She looked out at the snow swirling. Her heart thumped madly in her chest, like a landed fish beating against the gunnels of a boat. Then a peacefulness overtook her, a resignation. All the things she expected had finally come home to roost, fresh and gleaming in their innocent arrival. She wasn't crazy. He was truly a liar.

Emptiness slid around her like a pair of cold arms.

But it was okay. Things were clearer now.

She picked up the two halves of the condom wrapper, went around to the front seat and laid them neatly on the dash. Then she threw the keys on the seat, locked and slammed the door and walked away from the car, toward her own, opened the creaky door, took the key from her pocket and turned it in the ignition.

*Click.*

*Click. Click.*

She got out of the car and walked away from the apartment building, out on to the road, and home.

PART III

# MARY & RANDY

## ❧ Seventeen

THE SIGHT OF HER. WASHED UP ON THE STEP LIKE AN ABAN-doned child in a basket of reeds. I knew better than to ask what was wrong.

It was late when she showed up. I peeked out from behind the bedroom curtain and saw her down below, knocking at the door like it wasn't her house anymore. I'd have been insulted if I hadn't been sick with fear, her standing there in the bitter wind, staring straight ahead and not having the sense to come in. I sailed down the stairs, unlocked the door and pulled her through. Her apartment was more than two miles away, but by the cold in her cheeks, she'd clearly walked the whole way.

I looked into my only daughter's eyes. They were dull and watery, from the wind or something else, I couldn't tell. She looked like despair had burrowed right into the very quick of her. Bottomless hearts feel bottomless grief.

I helped her take off her parka and went to the living room to get her a quilt. She stood stock-still. I pulled a chair from the kitchen table, and sat her down to take off her boots. Bare feet. White-tipped toes, cold as death. I slipped them under my shirt and held my breath as our skin touched. She stared over my shoulder toward the rocking chair in the living room, gently swaying from the release of the blanket. As her feet warmed, tears began to flow unwanted, uncontrolled down her windburned face.

*What did he do, Mary?* The words clamoured in my throat like anxious, snarling dogs.

I tucked the quilt under her feet and got up to put on the kettle. Once boiled, I loaded a mug with sugar and ginger and lemon, nudged her gently from her chair and walked her up the stairs to her old room. It looked foolishly young for her now, in the light of midnight, spat out from the mouth of adulthood. I found her old terrycloth robe in a drawer and laid it, along with her tea, on the bedside table. Then I kneeled at her feet, kissed her two folded hands and left, closing the door behind me.

We didn't speak a word.

## ❧ *Eighteen*

TOAST CRUNCHING, KNIVES CLATTERING: THE FAMILIAR SYM-phony of morning. Mary did not go to work the next morning, and Randy didn't ask why. He had more important things to do, like pass her the honey and top up her coffee. She was a healthy pink this morning, but the frightening dullness persisted in her eyes.

"You hitting the road anytime soon?" Mary asked, blowing the steam off her cup. The first words she'd spoken since she'd arrived.

"Hadn't planned on it." A half-truth. He was supposed to be leaving for Montana the next day to pick up a load of feed, but had cancelled the trip in his mind the moment he found her on the step. "Why?"

She set down her cup and ran her thumb up along the handle. "Is it all right if I stay here awhile?"

"As long as you like, Mary. Or need. This is your home."

"Thanks." Her eyes remained on her mug, then drifted laconically toward her breakfast.

"Not hungry?"

"Not really."

She reached for the coffee pot, and nearly dropped it. She pulled back her hand and cradled her wrist like a fallen bird.

"Baby, what's wrong?" Randy asked, taking her hand gingerly and rolling it over in his. On the underside of her wrist, on either side of her tendon, were two fading bruises, squared off like rival teams on the centre line. "What the hell is this?" All the fury of the night before, there again, suddenly caustic.

"Nothing," she said, yanking back her hand. "I caught it in a freezer at work."

"Nice trick. You're not only klutzy, but you're double-jointed, too? Those are fingermarks, aren't they, Mary?"

"I just told you what they are." She exhaled slowly, letting the air spill like water from between her lips. "I don't have the energy for this, Dad."

"Mary. Tell me what's going on over there." He looked at

her levelly. "Tell me, or I'll go over there and find out my own way."

"I told you, Dad —"

"*Mary!*" He pounded the table, and she jumped in her chair, the dullness startled from her eyes. She glittered at him dangerously, at once afraid and territorial. "Mary," he began again more softly, "you show up in the middle of the night, out of your senses and nearly frozen blue. I put you to bed without question. Now it's the next day, and it's rather hard to eat breakfast when I'm gagging on small talk. Will you please show me the courtesy of telling me *what in God's name* that man is doing to you?"

She tried to keep staring him down, but in a few heartbeats, her face softened and the tears came again. Her nostrils flared, and her lips pursed.

"Tell me, Mary."

Her two hands fell to her lap, and she hunched at the shoulders, all the fight gone from her. "He came home late last night and lied about where he was. I found a condom wrapper in the car. I didn't know what to do. So I came here. That good enough for you?"

Randy came around the table toward her, pulled up a chair and took her in his arms. He rocked her back and forth wordlessly. He kissed the top of her glossy head. "Oh, baby." She smelled like mangoes.

Mary started to sob.

"And I'm pregnant."

The rocking stopped.

MARY SPENT A WHOLE DAY OF QUALITY TIME WITH THE couch while Randy tried to give her as much space as possible, finding every excuse to putter in the garage, or go downtown for a washer or a screw he announced it might be useful to have on hand, just in case. He picked up a dart game in the afternoon after he caught himself thinking he'd have to start re-grouting the tiles in the bathroom just for something plausible to do. He came home to find Mary where he left her, staring at the ceiling, hands on her belly, grey as old linen. She hadn't left the house and no one had called.

But the heart tires of even the most persistent of sorrows, and eventually she got up and started moving around again.

On the last day of the year, Mary stripped the tree of its ornaments and lugged it out to the patio. She burned her old robe. Then she headed for the kitchen, cleaned out the fridge and organized the roundabout with all the cereals, throwing out the ones neither of them had touched since she'd left high school. She found an old box of cookbooks in the basement and reinstalled them on the shelf above the glasses where her father had begun to keep the phone book and unpaid bills and Christmas cards that would never be answered. She baked bread and an oatmeal cake from scratch. Then she mopped the floor, went to her bedroom and closed the door behind her. It was seven o'clock at night. She hadn't said a word all day. The house smelled of cinnamon. Randy spent the night alone in front of the TV with a six pack and watched the crystal ball fall over Times Square.

On New Year's morning, Randy woke to find Mary outside on the back deck. She had pitched a lawn chair atop a beautifully sculpted snowbank, and sat in her parka with a cup of coffee in her mittened hands and a quilt wrapped around her legs. Once in awhile, she picked up a pair of miniature binoculars in her lap to get a closer look at the waxwings worrying the red berries of the mountain ash Randy had borrowed from the banks of the river and planted when Mary was a small girl. Somewhere between a coo and a shiver, the fifty or so of them sounded like a flock of church ladies. It wasn't every year they came in numbers like this.

Randy had fixed himself some toast and was sitting at the table reading the paper when she came in. He tried to scoot his thrill under the table.

"The birds are great," Mary said casually as she breezed through the patio door, clumping snow on the rag mat. She sniffled and threw her ponytail back over her shoulder, adjusting the bright orange toque on her head.

"They probably thought you were coming on to them with head feathers like that," he said, grinning, not looking up from the paper.

"Shut up! This is yours, I found it behind your fine collection of Esso ball caps. You got stocks in the company?"

"I'm a truck driver. They accumulate. That's my hunting toque you've got. But I do have more taste than that, if you look around. How about a nice Canadiens toque?"

"Yeah right. I wouldn't wear that one around loaded guns in these parts."

She'd looked like she was going to fill up on coffee and head back out, but instead, she took off her boots and sat down with her father at the table. Her pyjama bottoms were tucked into a floppy pair of wool socks. He slid her his plate of toast, and she grabbed the last piece.

"Thanks," she said, dusting her fingers onto the tablecloth.

"You made it," he said, referring to the bread.

"No. I mean for letting me mope. For letting me come back."

He set down the paper. "Mary. This is your home. You're always welcome here, sweetheart."

She nodded and pursed her lips, like she hadn't quite prepared herself for this conversation. "Thanks. But I've been a shit lately. I haven't called. I haven't told you what was going on. I wanted to handle it on my own. I hoped things would change for the better at any time, so why bother going through all the whiny details, you know?"

She rubbed her wrist and gently circled her hand.

"Things haven't been going too well with me and Darren lately. I'm almost glad I found out about his little road trip. Gave me a convenient excuse to leave."

Mary laid her hands on the table, and drummed out a military beat. Then she stopped and looked at Randy. "I don't know what happened to this grand scheme of his to write that book. I can't even remember what it was supposed to be about, exactly. Something about his grandmother, how she was auctioned off, and how this was somehow acceptable. All I know is that every day, I'd leave him in bed and go to work, and come home to find him on the couch or gone, the house a mess, and no indication of what he'd done with his day. Then he'd launch into my job, calling it the vocation of high-school sluts, stuff like that. On good days, he said it like he thought I was better than that, which seemed to me a backhanded way of insulting Sara. Other days, it was just snide and mean in its own right. Like sitting on your ass all day earns you the right to shit on everybody else's life. It takes one mean son-of-a-bitch to use all that precious time to figure out what's wrong with everybody else."

Randy sat still. "What about the bruises, Mary?"

"In a minute."

She'd never said any of these things before, and it surprised her to hear all the words strung together. "I just let it go. I figured he was having a hard time getting over losing his job. He never called it that, mind you, 'losing his job.'

Somehow he always turned it into his choice to leave. Anyhow, it was funny in a twisted kind of way. Ironic."

A smile spread involuntarily across her face, like a storm cloud in a summer drought, welcome regardless of its source. She noticed Randy noticing it, and sucked it back into the pores of her skin.

"Then I missed a period. I waited five days. One afternoon at work, I grabbed a test off the shelf and peed in the cup. Sure enough."

"What did he say?" Randy braced himself for the answer, and put aside his anger at not being told.

"He doesn't know."

Randy stared blankly.

"I haven't told him." Mary's face was impassive. There was a slight blush on her cheeks, whether from the chill outdoors or the trial of retelling the story, it was impossible to tell. She sat back in her chair and folded her hands in her lap.

"Didn't he notice you hadn't had your period?" Randy asked awkwardly. This was not a conversation for which he — or any father — was prepared.

"He went for days without noticing whether I lived or breathed, let alone the state of my bodily functions. I was waiting for the right time."

They let the words hang between them for a time.

"What about the bruises, Mary?"

She took several quiet breaths and looked this way and that, as though searching for a missing script.

"He's got a short fuse. And a sick sense of humour." She seemed to hope that was enough. Randy waited for her to go on. She didn't.

"Dad, this is making me sick. I have to go lie down." She got up to leave.

"Mary?"

"What?"

"What are you going to do about the baby?" His mouth was dry and his tongue was beginning to fail. "Darren doesn't need to be involved, you know. I'll help you any way I can. I'll raise it like my own."

"Thanks, Dad. That's a bit weird. But thanks." Mary smiled weakly. "I don't know what I'm going to do. I'm only two months gone. I have a couple of weeks to decide."

Then she shuffled off to bed, already heavy with history.

## ❧ Nineteen

MARY SAT HUDDLED IN THE BALL-FIELD BLEACHERS BEHIND the apartment on Third Avenue and watched Darren through the window. If stalking him was the only way to get back some of her things without confrontation, then so be it. Her father had offered to go over with her and empty the place, any time, day or night. But she wasn't ready for that, and her father was the last person she wanted with her. He was as likely to torch the place with Darren in his bed as he was to politely hold open the front door.

The truth was, she wasn't sure she was ready to move out for good. She needed time away from Darren, certainly, partly out of a hunger for clarity, and partly out of curiosity.

She wanted to remove herself from The Context of Darren and see what still made sense. But she was too practical to dismiss Darren simply for breaking rules, even ones like fidelity and kindness; she thought human beings were more complicated than that. On the other hand, she also would not be made to look like a fool. All she knew right now was that she was too exhausted to make a decision about anything.

In the meantime, it had been two weeks and she wanted her sketchpad. It was Monday night, and the Kings were playing the Flames, which meant it was likely Darren would head downtown to catch the game somewhere the television was in colour and you didn't have to get out of your chair for a beer. She'd thought he would have left by now, but she could still see him flickering now and then before the window in a flame-orange shirt, and his hair a state. He made her mouth water even now, even here, in this humiliating situation, staking out her own apartment in the dead of a winter's night, wearing her father's hunting toque, and pregnant. Upon sober reflection, the hunting toque probably wasn't a stellar idea, but if she took it off now, they'd find her frozen stiff as a barber's pole in the morning. She grunted a single acerbic laugh and sniffled. How ridiculous. All of this. Her freezing two little hearts to death, and him in there no doubt chatting up his favourite little slut.

Darren would be a train wreck of a father. Even if he could bring himself to love someone who relied on him — who *required* something of him — he was reckless and selfish. This was, of course, if he even bothered to stick around. More likely, he would disappear and become an even greater liability as The Father Who Would Have Been. Either way, she was loathe to spend her life trying to steer the kid away from him.

Then there was the issue of future family. Having grown up a single child, she had always craved a large, raucous family, bushels of kids who saw themselves reflected in each other — multiple iterations of physical probabilities — the happy peace of a house full of softly sleeping arms and legs, noses and bums. Darren was not the man for that. Darren was a man whose family — if he ever had one — would happen to him by accident, drop in unannounced.

Mary buried her mittened knuckles in her eyes and shook her head. The issue now was not about her grandchildren's trust fund, it was about this little thing about to have fingers and toes in her belly. For all she knew, it might have them already.

The thought of it being *whole* stopped her heart for a moment. If she decided to keep the baby, she would have to be prepared to raise it on her own. For a lifetime. It struck her dumb with inertia. It would likely mean putting aside her paint, her notions of herself as a hip young chick, and probably even work.

She juggled all the possibilities, tried to harden herself against this already ferocious love she couldn't yet afford.

Presently, the light went off in the apartment. She waited a few minutes for Darren to make his way down the stairs and skip across the parking lot to the car. He looked up momentarily as he crouched into the front seat, but apparently the figure across the field huddled against the cold didn't register for very long, and he took off. Mary unfolded herself from her perch and walked slowly through the frozen grass toward number 307.

Inside, the television was on, with the sound down low. The Christmas tree was quietly disintegrating in the corner. There were empty cans of beef stew and tomato soup on the counter, old takeout styrofoam clamshells in the garbage. The kitchen table was covered with unopened mail, including a letter for her that had been doodled over with the name of a diner and a phone number. All the plants — except for the cactus, which was thriving — needed attention. The bed was unmade. The state of the toilet made her gag.

She dug through their bedroom closet for a few sweaters and a pair of overalls, the closest things to maternity clothes she could find. Halfway through the door she turned.

She couldn't.

She could.

She lifted off the blue comforter of her youth and searched the sheets for stains. Darren couldn't be trusted to tell the truth, but linen never lies. No stains that she could see. At least he'd had the decency to keep it out of her bed.

Mary smiled, and was suddenly proud that she could do so, despite everything. She attributed it to the hormones.

In the living room, she loaded her paints into their case and threw some CDs into an empty backpack she found poking out from under the couch. In the kitchen, she liberated the liquor cabinet of its contents, just to be bad. She took all the toiletries from the bathroom. She rifled through the mail for her things, leaving behind the bills. Not that it mattered — the phone and power were in her name.

The phone.

She dug through her bag for her letter with the scribbling on the envelope. Dry Creek Café, 429-0318. She searched the front pages of the phone book for the source of the 429 exchange: Brooks. She picked up the phone and dialed *69. Then she hit the redial button and got the voice mail of one gum-chewing, too-cool-for-you Clare, complete with a thumping dance beat. *God love technology*, she thought. *You stunned bastard.*

Smug with her successful foray into private investigation, she hung up and was about to leave it at that. Then she knelt down and pressed redial again.

"Hi, you've reached Clare's voice slave. Leave a message and I'll get back to you when I can."

*That is, when I get off my back long enough to get to the phone*, Mary offered as an addendum. The machine beeped.

"Hi, Clare. I could be way off track here, but I'm guessing you were the little tart who soiled the back seat of my boyfriend's car a couple of weeks ago. I suppose I should thank you for making me see some things I might not have. Maybe I could impose on you for one more favour. Darren and I aren't really on speaking terms, so the next time you're talking to him, could you tell him I'm pregnant? Thanks. Toodles."

Mary hung up the phone and screeched with malicious joy. This was entirely too much fun.

"IT'S GOOD TO SEE YOU PAINTING AGAIN," RANDY VENTURED. He stood halfway in the room, timid in his own house. He was wiping his hands on a tea towel.

"Hey, Dad. Come in." Mary jerked her head toward a chair. "I'm not taking over, am I?"

"No. Well, yes." Randy strode toward the chair. "But I wouldn't have it any other way. It's nice to have a female around again. Reminds me to change the toilet-paper roll and water the plants once in awhile."

"I'm glad I appeal to your higher faculties."

"You know what I mean. How's it going?"

"Which, the parasite or the art?" she asked, squinting a little to blur the lines on the canvas. Then she looked up and grinned a wicked one. "Oh, wait a minute, I'd have to be more specific on *parasite*, wouldn't I?"

"The art."

"Okay, you know? It's been awhile. But it's coming back. It's like getting reacquainted with an old friend. I should have noticed something was wrong when I stopped thinking in colour. I don't think I did it intentionally. I guess it just started to seem like an invasion of Darren's space. How crazy is that?"

Randy bit his tongue.

"I raided the joint last night."

"What do you mean, you raided it?"

"I sat out in the ball-field bleacher behind the house and waited until he was gone. Then I went in and took a few essentials."

Randy shook his head slowly. "Don't you find it strange he hasn't called?"

"What? Oh, I don't know. He'd have to have something to say for himself then. And he probably knows you'd sooner put a bullet in his head than have to be civil to him."

"Mary. What would make you say a thing like that?" Randy's face contorted into mock outrage.

"Am I wrong?"

"Yes."

She cocked her head at him. "One hundred percent wrong?"

"Every bit of it."

She pursed her lips and nodded once, disbelieving him utterly.

"While we're on the subject," Randy advanced gingerly, like a man bellying over pond ice.

"Bullets in Darren's head?"

"Stop it. What about the baby?"

"The baby, Dad," she repeated, sounding to Randy too much like a young girl arguing for an extended curfew, "is not a baby. It's a fetus. I'll ask you to respect that important distinction, okay? Otherwise, my head will explode, and then you will have to clean up the mess." The voice of a nervous child. "I suspect it's doing fine. Free lunch, a warm place to sleep. What more could a parasite want?"

She put down her brush. Randy let her breathe.

"What do you think I should do?"

"Mary. You know I can't make that decision for you."

"I know. But you must have an opinion on the matter. I'm knocked up, Dad. This is going to become all too real all too quickly. I'm going to get fat and ugly and people are going to talk, then there'll be the baby and I won't be able to work and no one will touch me with a ten-foot pole and you will wind up supporting me. A young single mother, barely out of braces, on the bum."

He stared at her. Twenty-two years old, very nearly twenty-three. His baby girl, bearing the weight of the world.

"It's up to you, Mary," he said mildly. "I will make a fantastic grandfather. But there's plenty of time for that."

He got up out the chair, balled up the tea towel and

pitched it onto the counter in the kitchen. "I'm going to catch a game of darts downtown. Want anything?"

"Darren's head on a stick, maybe, if you see him and it's convenient. Otherwise, no thanks."

Randy kissed her on the forehead, found his coat and closed the door behind him.

## ❧ *Twenty*

ANOTHER COLD NIGHT, AND CLEAR. I DECIDED AGAINST darts in favour of a walk.

The snow crunched like gravel beneath my feet, and the air, gelled with cold, swirled behind my like the wake from a boat. The sound of a dog barking, of distant traffic. A siren.

How could I explain to Mary what I had lost when her mother had died on the birthing table? Should I tell her about the times I'd sat up at night holding her while she cried inconsolably, convinced she must know somehow what she had lost? How about the times I'd come home from a trip, relieve an aunt of her babysitting duties, then lie down with her in my arms, the two of us afloat on the familiar smells of home, and my heart would sting for the want of Ros' touch on the two of us? Or how the sight of a baby on the shoulder of its mother, with its tiny fists buried in her hair, could paralyze me with longing? How I'd felt something close to shame at her high school graduation, with all her girlfriends lined up with their mothers, sharing each others' features, as if every girl had been given a glimpse of her future, and Mary had only her bumbling father by her side, awkward as an unbroken horse. These were the spaces a missing mother leaves in a life.

Mary having this baby would privilege me with seeing what I'd missed and had tried in my clumsy way to replace. And if I could nurture Mary's turn at motherhood, maybe I could even make up for what *she* had missed.

I told her none of this. It was too much.

She still hadn't told me about the bruises. "A sick sense of humour," was all she'd said. It took fantastic leaps of faith and logic to think they might have come from anyone but Darren.

I was torn. I'd taken Darren on his word that he wasn't a violent man, contrary to what any person with a ten-year-old's dose of skepticism might have believed. I had ignored my gut out of sympathy. I'd fallen for charisma. I'd been had. That alone was enough to give any man a vendetta.

But now the boy was to be the father of Mary's child, and

that complicated everything. Maybe the responsibility would straighten him out. Maybe it wouldn't. Maybe he was reckless. Darren had to know I would kill him in a second for hurting my daughter. But maybe he was reckless *and* stupid.

I could go over there now and do it with no qualms. If it came to that.

I knew I was going to have to leave soon for a trip. I hadn't been out in weeks, and the numbers in my bank account were beginning to spiral. The company had called again about a feed trip into Montana; if I didn't take one of their offers soon, they'd begin to lose interest me. I didn't want to leave Mary alone right now, but it looked as though I might have to.

I walked to the edge of town, along the gravel access road next to the train tracks, which trailed off under the moon like two long finger tracks dragged through the sand. I took off my gloves and lay the palm of my hand on the cold iron, allowing the chill to ricochet up my arm and into my spine. Could a child's penny really derail a locomotive? I doubt it. It was a lie like all the others made up to drill the fear of consequence into an innocent mind.

Just then, I heard the *ting, ting, ting* of a dropping crossing bar. I stood up and looked for the dim stain of light appearing on the snowbanks around the curve in the tracks. Could they see me? Would they care? Sudden speed and danger.

I stayed put, my heart beating faster as the light swept

around the curve. I flinched. I froze. I sang with rage. I howled at the darkness.

Then I stepped down. The train sped closer and galloped by. And in the passing, only the ringing in my ears remained, with the echo of the crossing bell's last note.

## ❧ Twenty-One

MARY: PRESENT DAY

"GOOD RIDDANCE, THEN," MARY SAID WITH A GRIN. SHE leaned against the wall, arms folded over her chest, as Randy stood up from lacing his boots. He was flushed a little from the effort. "It's about bloody time you aired yourself out a bit. I was starting to think you might take up crocheting."

"Are you sure you're going to be all right? I've asked Auntie Margaret to look in on you, and help you with the groceries —"

"I'm pregnant, Dad. Not an invalid. Just how long were you planning to be away, anyway?"

"Not sure. I have a couple of side trips to make. A week

at the most. Think you can handle that? I can cut it short, if need be."

Mary looked at him under lowered eyebrows. "You'd think you were packing up for the winter, the way you were going on. Would you get out of here?" She kissed him on the forehead, then turned him around by the shoulders and shooed him toward the door. "Call me from the road," she said, as the screen door bounced shut behind him. "As if you need reminding."

She closed the door and smiled at her father from behind the glass. She continued watching as he walked down the steps, across the gravel driveway, then climbed into the cab of the truck and eased away.

MARY PUSHED THROUGH THE DOOR OF THE IGA WEARING high boots, a long wool coat and a garish scarf wrapped tightly around her head and neck. Sara thought she looked like a digitally retouched photo of a Czech immigrant. The image made her smile.

"Hey, you! Good to see ya. Come here." Sara opened her arms, hugged Mary and pulled her into the warmth. She breathed in the smell of cold and wiped the bangs out of Mary's eyes. She shuddered and pulled her white clerk's jacket tight over her body. "It's bitter out today. How've you been? Miss this place?"

Mary released the top button of her coat, loosened her

red scarf and let it fall through the air like a flag.

"Oh, my God! What did you do?"

"It's just a haircut," Mary said with a shrug. "I needed a change."

Sara turned Mary around slowly, like a cake on display in a baker's window. The layers of her hair were mangled, the edges uneven. "This come with a warranty?"

"I did it myself. Not bad, eh?" Mary asked over her shoulder.

"You did what?" Sara turned Mary to face her. "What on earth for?"

"I don't know. I was just standing over the sink last night, and it occurred to me that I needed a change. You can't tell me you've never had the urge to pick up a pair of scissors and go to it."

"Well, yeah, but I also get the urge to jump from tall buildings and bridges."

"Good thing we live in the prairies."

Sara sighed deeply. "If you were that desperate, you should have called. I could have done it for you. Or at least found a pair of sharp scissors. What did you use? Wire cutters?"

Mary turned toward a glass cabinet and picked out her reflection among the packages of film and batteries behind the glass. "I don't know. I kind of like it. Hair was just starting to piss me off, you know? I'd go to sit up in bed, and it'd be pinned behind my shoulders. Or I'd walk outside without tying it back, and the wind would drag it down my throat. It was starting to cramp my style." Mary turned her face from side to side and poked optimistically at the back of her head. "It's boyish."

"I see," Sara said, and did. The truth was, Sara figured, Mary felt overwhelmed by biology. Cutting her hair was the easiest way to feel in control again.

"Here. Let me take your coat." Sara took the garment from Mary's shoulders, and folded it over the counter beside a stand of plastic grocery bags. "Want a pop?" She went to the back of the store before Mary could protest, and returned with a club soda.

"Thanks," Mary said, and clinked bottles with her.

"How are you feeling, anyway?" Sara said, opening her bottle, trying to appear casual.

"Tired. A bit sick in the mornings. Although I think that might be all in my head. It might just be the prospect of a new day with this belly full of ruination."

Sara watched Mary without smiling, then reached for her bottle and opened it for her. She passed it back without a word.

"Oh, Sara, I don't know." Mary's eyes were glassy and she opened them wide so as to dry away the threatening tears. "I just can't face any of it, you know? I come to one decision, then I live with it for five minutes, then I've changed my mind again. Whole afternoons can pass like that, you know?"

"Are you doing any painting or anything?"

"I'm trying. But I just can't muster any concentration. I get an image in my head, then I'm off imagining myself five years down the road with a kid — in *kindergarten*, for Christ's sake — doing laundry all day and looking forward to my one outing to the grocery store to compose nutritionally balanced lunches. Or instead, I'm off somewhere in Toronto or Montreal, lonely and miserable, and hating myself for missing the one chance I can never get back to have a child." Mary closed her eyes and dropped her head back. "I'm paralyzed by choice."

Sara reached to touch her, but Mary lifted her head and waved her away.

"It's my own fault."

"Takes two to tango."

"Darren? He can't be held responsible for his dick." Then she added as an afterthought, "Apparently."

"Have you told him yet?"

"No. Jesus. What good would that do? Probably just drive him away."

"Maybe that's not such a bad thing."

"Good point. No, I don't know. I'm really not interested in his opinion. This is something I have to decide on my own. I don't expect him to stick around if I have the baby. In fact, I kind of hope he doesn't. Or wouldn't. Or ... whatever. You know what I mean."

"Yeah."

"Maybe I should go away and have it. Make him think I've run off to become some low-rent bohemian. He'd get bored, leave town, then never think of me again. I could wait him out."

Sara crooked an eyebrow.

"Or not. You see what I mean? I'm hopeless."

"You're not hopeless. You're thoughtful." Sara stretched a hand toward her knee. This time Mary didn't flinch. "And you're a smart girl. You'll make the right decision."

Mary lay down her pop and began to put on her coat. "What day is it?"

"Monday."

"Right. That means Tina's off work. Dad's out of town on a trip. Why don't you two come over for supper tonight?"

"Great idea! I'll call Tina."

"Okay." Mary began wrapping the scarf around her head, then stopped. "Did you say you had a pair of sharp scissors?"

"THAT, MY DEAR, IS MUCH BETTER." TINA STOOD AT ARM'S length from Mary with a half-glass of wine in her left hand, a towel in her right. "A little secretarial for my taste. But at least you don't look like you messed with an auger and lost.

I just can't imagine what you were thinking. You might want to keep your artistic yearnings on the canvas from now on."

She held up a mirror. Mary looked this way and that, running her fingers along the sharp new edge of hair. "My neck is cold," she said a little uncertainly. Then she giggled and reached for her wine. Sara grabbed the bottle from her and topped up her own glass before pushing it along the table.

"It's only hair. It'll grow back soon enough," Sara said.

"Indeed. I'm just a regular pot of fertilizer these days," Mary said, cocking her head in a shrug.

"Enough of that. It's all been decided now, no more," Tina scolded, setting down her own glass and reaching under the kitchen table for her bag.

"I suppose it has," Mary said, downing another slug of wine.

"It'll all be over before you know it. Then you can get on with the rest of your life and forget about the asshole. Leave him to the dogs, my dear. Now come over here to the sink. Where do you keep the plastic bags?"

## ✤ Twenty-Two

BEING ON THE ROAD AGAIN WAS GOOD FOR ME. WINTER wasn't necessarily the best time of year for driving. Snow squalls could rise up out of nothing, and the black ice was like a predator lying in wait to pick the weakest from the pack. And the four-wheelers had a deathwish like no other time of the year. They were like high-school thugs with their coats unzipped to their navels, tempting winter's temper. They'd pull around you in the heaviest storm, the snow coming horizontally. Or they'd crawl up your ass and take cover from the elements. Like flies, they were, buzzing, biting flies.

And the wind across those bald-assed prairies. Like it

had blown forever and was only just getting geared up. Guys had the roofs torn off their rigs. Made a person want to carry a trailer full of concrete, just for ballast. And you worried more about breaking down. A person on a back road alone had better have enough supplies to build a small field hospital. I still had my CB radio to call out. But with cell phones and CD players, it was getting so that people didn't turn them on so much anymore.

But winter was also the time of empty, velvety fields and snowy owls. I loved the way they stared at you from ragged power poles like they'd been expecting you for days. I loved the way fences stood out like zippers, or stitches. I loved the whiteness of it all. The rippling stillness. It sunk me into a state of meditation normally pushed aside in my daily recipe of errands, conversation and other bite-size portions of living. There was no denying one's own company on the road. Sailors and lighthouse keepers must feel the same way.

There was also something decidedly seductive about driving south, something I'd never been able to explain or deny. The air changed the moment I gave my last nod to the U.S. border guards. It became more dangerous. More immediate. When I was there, in America, the plot truly began. It was a symptom, I know, of a Canadian's homely-little-brother syndrome, but it kept me going back all those years.

AROUND TWO O'CLOCK, I FOUND AN ALL-NIGHT ESSO AND pulled off behind the diesel station and the propane tank. I stepped out into a night as cold and crisp as a hundred-dollar bill. A thousand miles north of here, the northern lights would be huffing across the sky, harassing the coyotes into fits of mad yelping. I crossed the parking lot and passed a line of other slumbering rigs like so many wagons circled. There were a few other cabs with dim lights on in their upper windows and I thought briefly about knocking on one for company. Instead, I bought myself a Coke in the convenience store, then retired to the cab of my truck.

I climbed upstairs and slipped my hand under the mattress for a cold, metal, vaguely sickle-shaped container. I slugged back part of my pop, added a healthy splash of whiskey, and poured it down my throat. I kicked off my shoes, lay back on the mattress and let the pleasant burn take over my throat and belly, and work its way into my fingers and toes.

I'd pulled out of Great Falls at midnight with four tons of chicken feed, and hauled two-hundred miles. I'd be crossing the border first thing in the morning. But now that I'd hit my stride, I was in no particular hurry to get home. At times like these I felt I could drive forever, nothing but the sky above and my truck wrapped around me, familiar as my own left arm. How many times with little Mary beside me had I been tempted to just keep driving in a straight line until we ran out of highway or horizon, whichever came first? But we always had to get her back for something. A doctor's appointment. A birthday party. Shopping for the first day of school. Or maybe it was just to check in with my sisters, to prove I wasn't making a mess of everything.

I'd taken the long way down again, through the mountains, for nostalgia's sake. In Choteau, I was saddened to find our old motel boarded up, the neon sign long extinguished. The highway seemed long and utterly desolate, as though no one had ever driven it before and no one ever would again. Red eyes swirled in the darkness as horses shied at the side of the road.

Maybe I'd been wrong. Maybe we never had to get home for anything at all. How different would things have been had we just kept driving?

I finished my drink, pulled off my boots and shirt, and slipped in under the quilt for the night.

## ❧ Twenty-Three

RANDY SLEPT IN AND A PROTEST AT THE BORDER SLOWED things down considerably. He didn't pull into Lethbridge until around eight and it was still another several hours before he'd be home. He could push on through or take his time, spend the night and still make it into Edmonton in time to off-load tomorrow. He decided to stop for a bite to eat and see how he felt later.

He stepped through the door of the Town Crier Restaurant and Lounge and rubbed his hands against the cold. A young couple, barely old enough to read, it seemed, hunkered in a booth in the corner under a low-slung green lampshade. Four guys lumbered around the pool table on the other side, amassing a table of empties. A large man in a bright shirt was smoking at the counter, bent over a glossy magazine advertising fishing gear.

"Grill still open, do you know?"

The man looked up from his magazine, squinted and stubbed out his cigarette. He looked at the clock behind the bar. "Yeah. Another half-hour." He fished in his pocket for a package of Craven A, and offered one to Randy.

"No, thanks."

"Suit yourself," the man said, and turned back to his magazine.

A waitress slunk by and slid Randy a menu. "Another one, Kitchener?" The man at the counter nodded and she ducked around behind the bar to get his Budweiser.

"Avoid the liver," the man said without looking up. He belched, his back bouncing involuntarily.

Randy looked sideways at him. "Thanks."

The waitress returned with a bottle of beer. Randy ordered a bowl of soup and a clubhouse sandwich. Then, as an afterthought, a whiskey and Coke.

He smoothed down the legs of his jeans and blew into his hands again.

"What brings you here?" the man asked, again without looking up from his magazine. Randy began to wonder if he had some kind of neck problem.

"Just passing through."

"What are you, a salesman or something? Missionary?"

"No. I'm a truck driver. Just bringing back a load from Montana. Should be home tomorrow afternoon." *Or earlier, judging by the company*, he thought. "And you?"

"What?" The man crushed out another cigarette.

"What brings you here?"

"I live here." The man flipped a page. "Not the bar. I mean, in town here."

The waitress arrived not a moment too soon with Randy's order.

As Randy ate, he contemplated that there is something deeply satisfying about foods that would be the same whether they were prepared in a diner in Wichita, or a blind alleyway in an Uzbekistan market: no one can fool up a clubhouse sandwich. Once he had some food in him, Randy felt a bit more congenial.

"What's that you're reading?" he asked, wiping a smear of mayonnaise from his thumb onto a paper napkin.

"*Cosmo.*"

Randy stifled a laugh, and tried to make it sound like he was choking on a piece of lettuce. He took a swig of whiskey. This guy was too much.

"It's not what you think. I'm in the print business, myself. I admire the layout." He flipped the page to a sunburnished couple lying in a tangle of Indian cotton sheets.

"Uh-huh," Randy nodded. "What does that mean,

exactly, 'in the print business.'" He pushed a half-dozen french fries into a mess of ketchup.

"Newspaperman. I'm the editor of *The Western Voice*. Kitchener's my name." Kitchener closed the magazine, pushed it to the side and extended a hand toward Randy. His fingers were yellow with nicotine.

"Kitchener?" Randy wiped his hand on his jeans and took Kitchener's. "That's a strange name."

"It's my last name. That's all people go by."

"Like a sports thing."

"Kind of. How's the food?" He ogled Randy's plate. Randy paused, then waved toward it with an outstretched palm, as if to offer him some, but Kitchener waved it away. "What are you drinking there? You want another?"

Randy thought about it a moment, then shrugged. "Sure." He popped the last triangle of his sandwich in his mouth, and polished off the last of his drink.


"GET OUTTA TOWN! I THOUGHT THAT KID HAD DROPPED OFF the face of the earth! Or at least I hoped he had." Randy and Kitchener were on their fourth round when they discovered their mutual acquaintance: Darren.

"What do you mean? Darren leave you in the lurch when he quit or something?"

"Quit? Is that what he told you? I fired that kid's ass. He had pretty grand notions about himself. Seemed to think everything he touched should be Pulitzer material. Hadn't figured out the gig."

"Which is?"

"Selling ad space to people who buy the paper for catching the cat droppings and wrapping parcels."

"You take real pride in your work."

Kitchener rubbed his eyes hard with his thumb and forefinger. "Yes, as a matter of fact, I do. But it's pride in doing a job that exactly fits the circumstances. It's pragmatic."

"Right. So: Darren. You fired him?"

"Damned right. I don't suppose he told you about his illustrious past then."

"What do you mean?"

"You know, the old iron coffin."

"Oh, yeah. That came out the first night I met him, actually. I don't think he was planning for me to find out so early, but it kind of slipped out. He had talked about coming along on a trip, in fact, to do a story for your paper."

"Ha!"

"Maybe he never mentioned it. Anyway, I was kind of warming to the idea. Told him my next trip was into the States, and that he could plan to come on that one if he liked. But then he said he couldn't cross the border because of his record."

"Yeah, funny thing about those border guards. They just don't seem to like maniacal wife beaters. At least not the ones they can catch. I did him a favour by giving him a job. It was a little agreement I had going with a friend of his." Kitchener made a discreet toking motion and shrugged. "I figured writing a bit of copy every day was harmless enough."

Randy stopped. "Huh?"

"I thought you said he told you?"

"Yeah. His girlfriend left him for a guy who was beating on her, and he roughed the guy up."

Kitchener stared at him and shook his head slowly.

Randy grew slowly cold. "What are you telling me here, man?"

Kitchener said nothing for a time, then wiped his nose and sniffed. He dug a set of keys out of his pocket and shook them at Randy. "If you don't believe me, come read it for yourself."

KITCHENER FLIPPED ON THE FLUORESCENT LIGHTS AND immediately regretted it. He rubbed his eyes and wobbled over toward a metal cabinet beside a microfiche machine. "Pretty clever, eh? Got a government grant for this puppy." He patted the top of the monitor, then slid his hand along the bottom to power it up. He turned the keys hanging from the cabinet lock and ran up and down the binders on the shelves. "Not much call for it. But it saves keeping all that paper around. You never know when someone will want to go back and check an obituary or something. Ten years ago, it was. November, I think. I remember that because it was Grey Cup weekend." He tapped his temple. "Mind like a steel trap, when I want."

Randy sat down heavily in the chair in front of the unit, but was shooed away by Kitchener. "Out of the way, boy. You're about to see newspaper magic."

Kitchener opened the glass plates and slid in the murky acetate. He swooped around the surface, scanning the headlines, stopping to admire this ad and that with a satisfied *hmpf*. He took out the acetate, then tried another.

On the fifth try, he stopped. Then he stood up, and pointed Randy to the chair. "There you go."

It was a small article on page three. Randy froze.

*High River Man Charged with Attempted Murder. Nineteen-year-old Darren Boyce was taken into custody early Sunday morning after his nineteen-year-old girlfriend was admitted to hospital with two broken ribs and several bruises. Police arrived at 14 Willow Place to investigate a complaint of disturbing the peace, and found the man sitting on the couch with a baseball bat, and the woman in the bathroom. Boyce will be held in custody until his court hearing. The woman's name has not been released.*

"The writing's a bit straight ahead. Lately, I've been getting the reporters to jazz it up a bit when they can."

Randy stood up and walked out.

## ❧ Twenty-Four

DARREN TINKLED HIS BEER GLASS ABSENTLY WITH HIS PEN and scratched the bridge of his nose. He felt like a kid with homework. A kid with homework, a pint of stout, a room full of people with lives in various states of decay and a big screen TV, but a kid with homework nevertheless. He'd been trying to get down some ideas at home, but like nesting in the jaws of a sleeping python, it hurt when he moved. How many years had he gone to the news event of the day, then come back to the office to barf out a story in time to make it home for supper? Picking the words, telling the story, was not only his job, it was who he thought he was. This should not be a problem.

But the story was simply too big. And too much his own. It's easy to write another man's story, and say, *That's all I had.* Now that he was limited only by his ideas and capacity for hard work, he was scared. Ideas would appear to him in flashes, then stagger and falter when he tried to write them down. Phrases would appear and mesmerize him like a child with something shiny. He couldn't move. He'd gone to the bar for a change of scenery.

As usual, the bar was filled with fascinating behaviour. Women talking to women as if their lives depended on it, glancing over each other's shoulders for the next person coming through the door. Husbands and wives ignoring each other's identical laughter. Women trying to look serene and smart, fading into the wallpaper. A crooked old drunk screaming out, as though his kitchen was filled with greedy youngsters. Though Darren didn't yet know how, he was certain all of this would be useful to him in time. It was like window-shopping.

The purchase he wished to make was a young red-haired item at the bar in an unseasonably short skirt. He'd seen her before. She was the new teacher up the road, fresh from music school in Calgary. Rumour had it she'd given up an off-Broadway show to work on an affair with a married professor, but Darren had a feeling she was so naturally glamorous that people were simply compelled to make up stories about her.

She was there with the terminally single school secretary, who, he thought, wouldn't be half bad-looking if someone would only tip her off about the white loafers. The two women were flirting with their wine spritzers, trying to find something to talk about besides work. Darren wanted to rescue the redhead, and have her show him her gratitude, perhaps in the comfort of his own bed.

Then, like flood waters rising, came Tina.

"Working hard, eh, Darren?" she said from over his shoulder, gesturing toward his empty pad of paper. "If you keep this up, we'll be able to write off part of your bar tab as a charitable donation to the arts. Maybe we could get you a chair made up, with a little plaque with your name on it for the back. You could be writer-in-residence, and —"

"Shut up, Tina." He didn't bother moving his head.

"So how is that book coming, anyway, Darren? Any publishers interested yet, any big advances coming your way to, I don't know, pay a rent cheque once in awhile? You've got quite the set-up over there. You breeze into town with a big story and big attitude, Mary's old man sets you up so she'll at least have the basic requirements of life, you chase her out, and oh, look at that! Your own little country whorehouse, courtesy of your girlfriend's father. Pretty clever."

Tina laid down her tray, folded her arms across her chest, and bent down so that her face was inches from Darren's. She smelled of peppermint and citrus perfume and her cleavage plunged, making him ache like he'd been slapped in the face.

"You're nothing but a scam artist," Tina continued. She lowered her voice menacingly. "I've seen the bruises. Mary must think I'm a two-year-old, trying to sell me those little domestic-accident explanations. Let me tell you something, asshole. You touch her again," Tina sculpted the words with faintly smiling lips, "and I *will* kill you. I will kill you slowly, and with great pleasure. Do we have an understanding?"

Darren drained the last of his glass and stood up. "You know, Tina? You'll start to get a reputation, talking like that." He put on his jacket and slipped his notebook in the pocket.

Tina stopped him as he turned to go. She took another step forward and kept her voice low. She cocked her head in a kind of taunt. "I suppose you knocked her up to extend your time share, huh?"

Darren searched her face for the punchline, the explanation. The truth slowly filtered through to him.

"Three months," she went on, struggling now to appear unfazed. She knew it wasn't her place to be saying anything, but watching him sit there all smug and cocksure made her rigid with anger. She couldn't help herself.

"And when was she planning on telling me about it?"

Tina smoothed down the panels of his jacket, then gently placed a finger in the hollow of his throat and pushed.

"Pal, you have lost every right to a say in Mary's life. Try to muster the decency to stay away and let her decide."

He pulled her finger away from his throat and left the bar, forgetting all about the music teacher, at least for a moment.

THE NIGHT WAS BITTERLY COLD. DARREN WAS CERTAIN HE could feel the air enter his lungs and freeze the blood out to the tips of his fingers. But he decided to walk home anyway. The antifreeze in his veins would serve him well. The sky was filled with stars like black cloth held up to the sun, the Milky Way a fading frosty breath. The vastness of it all, ringing in his ears. He cursed Mary briefly for making him leave the svelte little teacher sitting impotently at the bar.

Pregnant? How could Mary be pregnant? He thought they'd been careful. He was sure, even. Well, mostly sure. The booze did it to him sometimes. The first time he'd had to ask Mary if they'd had sex the night before, she looked at him like he'd just killed her cat. She was so sweet. And so naive. But he thought she'd been paying attention, at least. She had the most at stake in this, after all. Maybe she'd done it on purpose. A surge of something like anger, something like fear, and something even a bit like joy overtook him briefly. He buried his chin deeper in his jacket and quickened his pace.

This had to be a dream. He'd had it before, marching sure-footedly along a seashore path that eventually became narrower and steeper, until he'd found himself perched on a sliver of stone, unable to move in any direction, painted into his corner by his own non-observance and forward momentum.

At Windemere he took a surprise turn left. He'd had little interest in Mary since she left, thinking she wouldn't be worth talking to until she'd cooled off anyway. But now he thought she had some things to answer for. He shuffled through the freshly fallen snow to Sylvan Lane, turned right, and planted himself before her bottom step. The light was on in her room, and nowhere else in the house. She was likely alone, or at least Randy was sleeping. He would go in.

He tried to knock; he couldn't.

Standing there in the light of the bare bulb outside the door, swaying like a barn door in the breeze, he found he was drunker than he'd realized. He could imagine her standing there in an old shirt pinched from Randy's closet, puffy-eyed from straining for sleep, her mute accusations throbbing in his bones. Maybe she'd even have a little belly by now. It had only been a couple of weeks since he'd last seen her, but it was hard to know how these things worked. Sometimes he wished she would just scream at him and get it over with. God knows he could handle confrontation much easier than extortion by silence.

Her eyes. The way she'd started to look at him as though he'd melted and reformed into something sinister, foreign. The confusion. As though she'd been betrayed. He hadn't meant her any harm. He hadn't thought her so fragile — her spirit so easily broken, her flesh so easily bruised.

None of this was supposed to happen. Juniper Butte had been a happy detour, lime green panties under a Catholic girl's dress. Surprising. Temporary.

The light switched off in Mary's room. Darren shifted in the snow, realizing how conspicuous he must look in the late night lamplight, staring at a door like it might open its mouth and begin to speak. How had things slid this far? The fabric on his coat threatened to crack with the cold. A dog barked in the distance, and though he knew the door to the house would be open, he thought briefly about finding Randy's hunting gear in the garage and crawling into a sleeping bag. His eyes itched with fatigue. He thought about creeping upstairs in behind the soft curve of the would-be mother of his child and kissing away the pain, of coaxing loose the Gordian knot hanging over them all.

Then he imagined Randy's itchy trigger finger in the next room, his breaths filling the air in the house with blue rage, and he changed his mind. Then behind him, a loud crack, like wood splitting, or the sudden fury of a rifle. He couldn't be sure what it was, but the dog had suddenly stopped barking.

What was he thinking?

Women with children, he reminded himself, were snivelling bores. They couldn't help it; the hormones brought it out in them. Pregnancy had made Sandra hopelessly clingy and demanding: no wonder they called it "expecting." His own mother was no better, and with her, the transformation was complete: she stayed that way her whole life. There was no reason to believe Mary would be any better. And what sort of gift was having a baby anyway? Anyone could do it.

Darren found himself swaying in acerbic drunkenness before the door. He blinked, opened his eyes momentarily wider, raked his ice-cold fingers along the slopes of his cheeks and tried to come to. Just then it hit him. He'd done it again. His mother. Sandra. Mary. An unholy trinity of neglect. Nausea rippled in his stomach and he staggered against the door frame. He could stop this now. All he needed to do was knock, ask forgiveness, and fall into two warm arms. Brave the next eighteen years. People did it all the time.

No. He simply couldn't face it. Mary would be in good hands.

Besides, he had a little something waiting for him in Brooks.

# ❧ Twenty-Five

I WAS TOO DRUNK TO DRIVE WHEN I WOBBLED OUT OF *The Western Voice*. I crashed in the sleeper of my truck and didn't wake up the next morning until eight, then cursed myself for it. I stopped into the Town Crier for a Danish and a cup of instant coffee to go, and then I was off, creaking into action despite the mighty inertia of my hangover.

Fifty miles into the drive, I hiked up my jeans and wagged my legs back and forth on the truck seat. The morning was bright, and the combined heat from the glass and the vent was starting to block out the sound, make the road swim before me. I opened the window and pried apart my eyelids, shifted in my seat, and took a deep breath of frost and dust.

I should have known the guy was bad news when Mary starting ignoring her art for him. I should have listened to my gut the first time it became apparent Darren was no more interested in carrying his weight around the house than joining the seminary. At the very least, I should have listened to Len.

The hills outside rolled by unendingly, like little sighs in a flat calm sea.

Now what?

I definitely had to get this guy out of the picture, there was no question of that. But if Mary was going to have the baby, I guessed she'd want the father around, if for no other reason than show. Or Darren might use the baby as an excuse to hang around on the gravy train.

Whatever Mary was going to do, she would need to make a decision soon. I couldn't imagine the state of suspension she'd placed herself in, waiting to decide if the thing inside her would live, waiting to decide if she'd let herself start calling it a baby. Waiting to decide if she could love this consequence of a sinister impersonation of love. If she loved the outcome, did I have to love the circumstances that bore it? Would it become a world-sized wedge between her and Darren, or worse, would it be an arm's-length chain keeping Darren always within swinging distance? All this wondering, while the thing grew dangerously close to having its own say in the matter.

I cracked the window and let the cool air spill over my face and thrill the skin on my arms into goosebumps. I turned up the heater a notch, and did my best to will away the next three hundred miles.

I thought of Ros. Of Sandra. Of all the skin shed in the name of possession. How women slip away. How they wilt. How life wants to live, and does, even under the gravest indignity.

*Rage.*

The sun glinted off the barrel of my rifle and I knew what I would do.

## ✢ Twenty-Six

TINA AND MARY SAT IN THE PLASTIC BUCKET CHAIRS AT THE clinic, making brave attempts at out-of-body experiences. Sara had to work and probably wouldn't have had the heart to come anyway. Mary fiddled with her newly red hair — "Scarlet Letter," the box had read — and leaning forward with her elbows on her knees, flipped through a three-year-old copy of *National Geographic*, the pages rippled from some kind of ancient wetting (the details of which were best not thought about in a medical clinic). She searched the photos for peoples' eyes, drawn in by the bottomless browns and pained blues, pale with disease. No one ever seemed to be having fun in this magazine, and if they were, it was only in the interest of propagating folk culture. She imagined the magazine's story meetings, all the editors and writers and photographers dusting themselves off from the belching breath of a volcano, or the wreck of an earthquake in a workers' slum, or whatever Important World Event they'd just returned from, shaking out their Tilley hats and adjusting their wire-rimmed glasses to fold their hands on the table.

"Mary Thompson?" A dangerously thin woman in white platform shoes appeared, file folder in hand. She was angular and bony, insect-like. A walking stick.

Tina turned to Mary and grabbed her hand. "That's me," Mary said, dropping the magazine on the next chair and rising timidly to her feet. The two women stepped hand-in-hand toward the nurse.

"Only Mary," the nurse said, reaching a protective palm toward Mary's shoulder.

"No, no. Mary wants me with her," Tina said, blocking the woman's hand. A red-eyed girl and her broad, angry mother in the corner of the room glanced up.

"I'm sorry. Mary will have to come on her own," the nurse reached for Mary again. Mary looked at Tina like a child leaving on a train, her bright hair somehow hilariously incongruous with the situation.

Tina shook her head ever so slowly and let her go. She thought she saw the smallest shudder go through Mary's sparrow shoulders as the walking stick led her away. "I'll be right here if you need me," she called out. Mary turned a corner and disappeared.

Tina sat heavily in her chair, picked up the magazine Mary had been reading and threw it down again.

RANDY SCREECHED INTO THE PARKING LOT BEHIND MARY'S old apartment and threw the truck into "Park." He hopped out of the cab, unlocked his rifle from the rack, slipped it down his pant leg and up under his sweater. He slammed the truck door behind him, searching through the keys on his ring for the one he knew he'd done well to keep a copy of. He took the stairs two at a time. The door stood open at the end of the hall.

He entered and looked around the apartment. He hoped like hell Mary hadn't been living like this: empty cigarette packages, half-empty bottles of beer on the speaker stands, drawing paper strewn like papers for a puppy, marked over in angry red marker, a woman's handbag leaning against the couch. And the cactus, resplendent in its abandonment. He padded softly down the hall: shag carpet was good for stealth, if nothing else. If Darren were there, he'd put the poor cur out of his misery. One shot to the head. Wouldn't know what hit him. It would almost be an act of charity.

Except for the stinking flotsam of his life, there was no sign of Darren. Randy walked out into the hall, checked the broom closet, then the kitchen. Nothing. Even the computer was gone.

Randy stood in the abandoned living room, the gun growing heavy in his hands. His knees buckled and he fell to the couch. The sobs came slowly and deeply, like warm oil rising over his body.

AT HOME, THE WIND CAUGHT THE DOOR AND SLAMMED IT shut behind him.

"Mary?" he called to the empty kitchen.

No answer.

"Mary!" Randy called again, wiping his boots on the mat, and feeling a sudden sense of urgency. He listened. Nothing.

He strode through the kitchen and rounded the bottom of the staircase, hauling himself up by the banister.

Her bedroom door was closed. He knocked quietly. "Mary?"

He let himself in. The curtains were drawn, but in the dim light he could make out a head with short, flame-red hair, on the pillow. Mary's body, curled into a question mark, was outlined under a thin quilt.

Randy was confused. "Mary? Is that you?"

"No, it's the Avon lady." She tried to laugh, and failed.

He sat down gently on the edge of the bed and lay his hand on Mary's shoulder. She was burning with heat. She rolled over. Her eyes were red-rimmed and great dark circles spread beneath. "Hi, Dad." She smiled weakly.

He caught his breath and his blood suddenly pounded in his ears. He searched her pale, tired face. "What happened to you?"

She closed her eyes, already exhausted by the conversation. "Just a little makeover, Dad. I thought I needed a change." She offered a flimsy smile. "What do you think?"

"Never mind the hair. What happened?" He was angry now and shook her a little. Tears began leaking from the corners of her eyes and rolled down her cheeks and past her ears as they'd apparently been doing all morning — her pillow was stained with a wet grey on either side of her head. She didn't seem to have the words.

"Mary." He tried to keep his grip from tightening on her shoulders. "Please, honey."

Still nothing. Then she swallowed with difficulty, and parted her parched lips. "I couldn't go through with it."

Randy leaned down to look into his daughter's eyes.

She blinked slowly and scanned his familiar face; it was too close to take in everything at once. Her father slid his arm under her neck and lifted her carefully to him.

Outside, a single blackbird lifted from a fence post.

# ❧ *Epilogue*

*Dear Ros,*

*This is foolish, I suppose, writing you a letter. You're in my head all the time anyway. And I suppose I'd be locked up if anyone caught me doing this. But there are a few things I wanted to tell you.*

*First, Darren never did come back. Never did call. Thank the four strong winds for small mercies.*

*I bought Mary and her little Rose a small house on the edge of town. And I built Mary a studio there. It's not much, really. Just a place with four walls where she can go and close the door — no argument. But it's in the north corner of the house for the painter's light, and it looks out over a garden of snap peas and pumpkins. Those buggers grow faster than Rosie can run. Rich ground, I suppose. Mary has started on a series of portraits. Maybe you could find Peter up there where you are and let him know, eh?*

*She has your eyes, Rose does. And your name.*

*Your Randy*

# ❧ Acknowledgements

THIS BOOK WENT INTO A LONG SLUMBER AFTER ITS FIRST draft, while the list of people who shaped it grew and grew. Thanks to my agent, Anne McDermid, and my editor, Lynn Henry, for signing on to something that was to become something else entirely. Undrea Norris opened up her studio to show me a thing or two about painting. The words in Mary's painting of the bird are taken from Steven Lattey's "A Snake Story," published in the anthology *Eye in the Thicket* (Thistledown Press, 2002). Terry Whitefield gave me a glimpse of the complex nature of a father's love; that glimpse was crucial to this story. Thanks to George Morgan, who believed long before mere mortals should have. Life on Chapel Street wouldn't be the same without Michael Cummey's encouragement, tequila, and enviable house parties, nor without the excellent community of writers and other artists in this town. Thanks to Colin Carrigan for keeping the fire stoked. To everyone else — and you know who you are — I am none of this without you.

## ❧ About the Author

MONICA KIDD grew up in Elnora, Alberta, and studied biology at the University of Calgary and Queen's University. She now lives in St. John's, Newfoundland, where she works as a broadcast journalist. She is also the author of the novel *Beatrice* (Turnstone, 2001). Her poetry has been published widely in Canadian literary journals.